About the Author

Garry Serafin grew up in western Canada and earned an M.A. in Comparative Literature in Quebec. After teaching for three years in a Cree community on James Bay, he moved to Switzerland where he studied translation and worked in business before settling into a career as a translator, mainly in finance.

The Cold War

Garry Serafin

The Cold War

Olympia Publishers
London

www.olympiapublishers.com
OLYMPIA PAPERBACK EDITION

Copyright © Garry Serafin 2023

The right of Garry Serafin to be identified as author of
this work has been asserted in accordance with sections 77 and 78 of
the Copyright, Designs and Patents Act 1988.

All Rights Reserved

No reproduction, copy or transmission of this publication
may be made without written permission.
No paragraph of this publication may be reproduced,
copied or transmitted save with the written permission of the publisher,
or in accordance with the provisions
of the Copyright Act 1956 (as amended).

Any person who commits any unauthorised act in relation to
this publication may be liable to criminal
prosecution and civil claims for damage.

A CIP catalogue record for this title is
available from the British Library.

ISBN: 978-1-80439-023-8

This is a work of fiction.
Names, characters, places and incidents originate from the writer's
imagination. Any resemblance to actual persons, living or dead, is
purely coincidental.

First Published in 2023

Olympia Publishers
Tallis House
2 Tallis Street
London
EC4Y 0AB

Printed in Great Britain

Dedication

For my parents, who are portrayed here much as I remember them.

Acknowledgements

I wish to thank my brothers and sister for their help in remembering details about Churchill that to me were long forgotten.

Part I

Danny

"I found him helping his mother at The Bay."

Dad's voice startles me out of my reverie and for a second, I can make no sense of it. What's he doing here at school? He's speaking to our teacher, Miss Sadler, from the back of the trailer that serves as our fifth and sixth-grade classroom. His tone is level and matter-of-fact, but clearly he's waiting for an answer. My classmates have fallen silent. Turning around, I gulp down a rush of anguish: there he is holding Moses, one of the two Chipewyan children in our class, by the collar of his jacket. I glance ahead and sideways to see if Jeff, Robin or (worse) Cynthia might be looking at me, but they aren't. Danny, seated in the desk behind mine, is doodling in the corner of his exercise book.

Miss Sadler pushes up her glasses and huffs in disdain through her freckled nose. "Take your seat, Moses," she directs, adding an officious, "We'll do what we can with him," for her own benefit. She pauses just long enough to exchange civilities with my father, who thankfully seems in a hurry. Wheeling about, he wishes us a good day over his shoulder. "My regards to Mrs. Swiantek," Miss Sadler calls after him as he bangs the door shut against the wind. I wince. "Now, class…" She continues where she left off, taking no further account of Moses, who has hidden his face in folded arms on his desk. She is eager to quiz us on the story we read for homework, about a boy saving up for a gleaming blue and silver bicycle in the display-window of a sports shop, somewhere far away down south. The story has a moral about thrift. They always had a moral, I will recall so many years later on, when I finally get down to writing this. Now, however, it merely occurs to me that there are few bicycles in Churchill. It is October 1963.

I note with relief that the others are unfazed by the interruption. Dad, as the new Indian agent, has already become a familiar figure around town. Not as familiar as Jeff's father, our bad-tempered school janitor, who shuffles around in his tattered striped sweater with the patched elbows. Nor as familiar as Robin's father, the RCMP sergeant, whose towering figure so flusters me that I can't lift my eyes from the pistol strapped to his hip. Though even he can't match the notoriety of Cynthia's amiable dad, the bush pilot, who has lived in Churchill a lot longer than most people and recently flew my father to a fishing camp upriver. It crushes me out to think they might have talked about Cynthia and me while winging their way over the stunted black spruce.

Danny doesn't have a father. He lives with his mother, a Métis washer-woman, in the Flats by the harbour. He tried to keep this a secret at first but I found out soon enough, even before school started. We met the day after my family arrived from the south. I was exploring the jumble of rocks along the shore behind our house, one of two that stand next to the post-office building. The houses look disproportionately tall because, like everything else in Churchill, they're built on clapboarded posts or skids to avoid contact with the permafrost. Besides the front and back porches, our house has a small living room (where my sister Beth sleeps on the couch), two tiny bedrooms (one for my parents, the other for my brother, Dave, and me), a kitchen and a closed-off area at the back where there is a pantry, a cubicle with a honey bucket and a low shelf where Mom does the laundry and prepares our weekly baths, all in the same square aluminium tub. The toilet is smelly but otherwise marks a step up from the outdoor privy we had previously. There's even a good fairy who empties the pail every so often. Bathing on the other hand is dismal, not only because like most preadolescent boys I'm averse to soap but also because I tend to be the last one in the water, which by then has grown cold and murky.

The second house, identical to ours, is where Jeff lives. How they manage with five kids in the same space that we have is beyond me and, frankly, I prefer not to know. When I call there I stay on the rickety doorstep, loath to venture into the sour smell of cabbage and the bawling of Jeff's snot-nosed younger siblings who tear around in dirty underwear. We will hear a couple of years from now, when Jeff's family moves away, that they've wrecked the place. All the government-provided furniture will have to be thrown out, and when the cleaners come; they will find holes in the walls along with filth – even traces of excrement – right up to the ceiling. The federal building on the other side of our house looks smart in comparison. It houses the post office, the police station and other offices including Dad's. Next to it are the RCMP barracks where Robin's family occupies the upper floor. Robin is an only child. His clothes and his English are nicer than ours. His mother was a war bride.

As I said, I was exploring behind our house. It's on the edge of town and the only other building farther out, when I walked down our back steps that late-August morning, was a large brown-and-yellow log cabin with a totem pole in front (the community centre, called Caribou Hall, as I would soon find out). Otherwise, the area was stark and patched with flat rock outcroppings sloping down to the beach. This was flanked by twisted masses of boulders that lined the shore, all the way to the river to the left and as far as the eye could see to the right. My senses quickened as I surveyed the strange new surroundings and for a moment the pang of loneliness I felt over leaving my friends in Norton ebbed. The wan sun hung still in the vast dome of the sky like a lemon with no juice. The landscape looked hunkered down and stretched to the tautness of an onion skin, as if tugged by enormous weights suspended below the low horizon. Southern Manitoba was similarly flat under a hulking sky but there we had trees whereas here there were none, only a thin layer of scruffy vegetation that hugged the ground for dear life. And instead of grain fields, here it was Hudson Bay that sprawled into the distance.

I headed down to the beach and gazed out over the flat expanse of water. A chill wind blew stiffly, combing the dark blue swells into whitecaps and broadcasting a rank smell, that was odd to me, of seaweed and rotting shellfish. Three ships rode at anchor in the offing, silent emissaries from an invisible world beyond. Seagulls swooped, their raucous cries glancing off the arc of tortured Precambrian granite. As off the scaly back of a leviathan, I will think to myself many years hence, squinting at a picture taken near the same spot. A spiky shell peeped out of the tangle of driftwood at my feet. I picked it up between my thumb and middle finger and, with my other hand, removed the caked mud until the orifice was exposed. I held it to my ear. It was true: you can hear the sea inside. The faint resonance held me spellbound for a long moment. I listened intently for a hesitation, a pause for breath, but the sound continued to issue like a steady whisper. It was a bit spooky, the more so because of a creeping sensation that someone was watching me. I glanced around but saw no one. Confused, I set the shell down gingerly and strode to the edge of the bay. Keeping my feet dry on the pebbles I crouched forward, dipped my fingers into the icy water and pressed them to my lips. The salt taste was tangy but not unpleasant.

Still bemused by the whisper in the shell I stood up, crossed the beach and began picking my way haltingly over the huddled crowd of boulders. Many were flat on top and bunched together like oversized molars, making it possible to skip over the warren of recesses between them. Yet some of the gaps were too wide to straddle, and there I had to slide down to the matted algae on the gravel below before clambering up onto the next monolith. I usually slid down on my backside so I could keep a bearing on my next objective, still two or three hundred yards away: a low, crenelated stone wall I'd spied with excitement the day before.

Here and there, in hollows among the rocks, lay pools of the clearest water. Most were bordered by patches of soft, dank moss. Coming to one such pool, I was sizing up the distance across its shimmering surface, unable to decide whether it could be jumped, when Danny came up behind me out of nowhere.

"I wouldn't if I was you," he warned. "It's slippery on the other side."

Startled to hear a human voice, I spun around to see who it was. At the same time, I struggled to register what he'd said exactly because of his accent: his 'th's had an edge, like 'd's. Having grown up in a fairly homogeneous community of English farmers, this was new to me. I studied his face. His dark eyes met mine blandly, half hidden by a shock of thick black hair. He seemed about my age and wore faded denims. There was a gaping hole in the toe of one of his running shoes.

"Hi," I replied shyly, unused to making new acquaintances.

Few strangers visited Norton and fewer still with children. Casting about for something to add, I turned back towards the pool, furrowing my brow and studying the smooth slab of stone that sloped upward on the opposite side. It was slimy where the water had receded. Worse, the pool looked knee-deep.

"Yeah, you're right," I mumbled self-consciously, ashamed of my lack of foresight. I was keen to change the subject. "You live around here?"

"Near the grain elevators," he said evasively and quipped, "Where you goin'?"

"To that fort over there," I said, nodding towards the crenelated wall.

He frowned as he followed my gaze. "You mean the cape," he said. "The fort's on the other side of the river." Puzzled, I looked out over the muddled sweep of wind-worn rocks and scanned the shoreline across the mouth of the Churchill River, nearly a mile distant. A flat dark shape resembling a blunt pencil stroke protruded above the depressed horizon, dwarfed by the overarching sky. That must be the fort. "I'll show you where to go," Danny offered, gesturing to our left. "It's easier this way."

He started off, expecting me to follow, which I did, glad to be guided over the alien terrain. He wasn't much taller than I was but appeared to know the rocks like the back of his hand. He negotiated their contorted shapes with so little effort that he often had to stop and wait while I puffed and scrambled to keep up, banging my elbows and knees. I'd stayed too close to the bay, where the gaps between the rocks created a twisting maze that Danny skirted. Closer to town these spaces gradually filled with a thickening layer of sediment. Soon there were bright clumps of bearberries, their leaves already tinged with red, along with smatterings of late-blooming flowers and dwarf willows.

Interwoven with moss and lace-like tufts of lichen, this mosaic illuminated the grey patchwork of stone with a riot of colour –a boreal rainbow ranging from emerald to white to crimson to purple and from orange to yellow to lime green, then back to emerald. The effect was more stunning than lovely, more raw than sensual. The rocks were mostly low and smooth now, flecked with greenish-white lichen and occasionally bearing a picture, a name or some other inscription scrawled with chalk. One drawing depicted a smiling girl in a skirt. 'Fuck me', the caption read. I gave it a sidelong glance and was just catching up to Danny when we passed another, cruder drawing. The girl was naked this time and pointed to her crotch. Pretending not to notice, I started questioning Danny about Churchill. I was apprehensive about going to a new school with new classmates and a new teacher. He answered me in short snatches. Clearly, conversation wasn't his strong suit, though he seemed to relish the role of mentor. Whether out of mutual hunger for companionship or real affinity, by the time we reached Cape Merry a bond was forming between us.

    The cape disappointed. Only one rusty cannon kept a lonely vigil over the mouth of the river; the other embrasures were empty. A rectangular opening that might once have framed a door led into a small chamber in the middle of the wall: the magazine! I crawled inside, sat still and strained to picture tall ships like the ones I'd seen in pirate comics, their sails billowing as they swung round to fire blazing broadside salvoes. I remembered the gunners with their knotted headbands ramming shot down the barrels of their cannon, lighting the fuse while hurling abuse at the enemy and rushing to reload. But the silence in the magazine daunted me. It stripped the evil grins from the imagined pirates' faces and popped the speech balloons, laying bare the gloomy oppression of the dank, cramped space. I had to get out.

Danny was leaning against the stone cairn that stood nearby. He eyed me as I climbed clumsily over the wall to join him.

"What's this about?" I asked, inspecting the worn bronze plaque on the cairn, pockmarked by pot-shots.

"Read it and you'll see." He spat on the ground.

The plaque commemorated an expedition led by Jens Munck, a Danish sea-captain. I skimmed over the passage, eager for genuine heroics, but it turned out that Munck and his men had been trapped here by winter and nearly all had starved to death. I shivered, suddenly aware of the chill in the air and the barren waste around us. Danny must have sensed my consternation.

"They came from the sea. They didn't know nothin' about the land." Whether he meant this as compassion or criticism I couldn't say.

"Is the fort any more interesting?"

"I guess so," he shrugged. "There's lots more cannons and the walls are higher." He broke wind as he spoke, a long intermittent splutter that ended like a door opening on squeaky hinges. His expression remained inscrutable so again I hid my embarrassment.

"Can you show me round the harbour tomorrow?"

He brightened. "Sure. You goin' home now?"

"Yeah, I promised my mom to help unpack. We just moved here yesterday."

"I know," he said. "I saw you get off the train."

It was then I realized that Danny must have been following me over the rocks at a distance, waiting for an excuse to sidle up. Did he check out all the new arrivals his age? I had no way of knowing that as a "half-blood" in Churchill's harsh racial pecking order, he had no real friends.

When he called the next day, I was playing in my room and didn't hear him knock. I'd laid out the Meccano set, my favourite pastime, on the floor and was engrossed in the construction of a medieval tower and drawbridge. Mom answered the door. "Ben!" she had to shout twice before her voice routed the knights and fluttering pennants arrayed in my daydream. I rushed through the living room, pulling on my jacket, but it was too late. By the time I got to the front door I could see she'd already been plying Danny with questions. Why are mothers so nosy? "He says he's going to protect you," she announced with a wry smile while Danny shuffled his feet self-consciously.

"I can take care of myself!" I retorted, pushing past them down the steps.

"Don't go near the river!" Mom cautioned. "There's a strong current and the water is freezing!"

"We won't!" I yelled back. While bemused by the previous day's let-downs, I could still feel the thrill of perceived adventure stirring within me. We followed the road out of town and soon came to the grain elevators, a high central concrete building flanked by rows of contiguous silos. Two ships stood moored to the dock, their towering bows streaked with rust from their anchor chains. Both were dry bulk carriers with names that could have been English or Scandinavian. We watched for some time as wheat was spewed into the hold of one, while smelted ore was dropped thunderously into the bowels of the other, by a crane which scooped the slabs from a hopper car at the end of the railway siding. We wanted to get a closer look at the crane but a swarthy man in a sweat-stained shirt told us with a gruff voice to stay clear.

"You knew that guy?" I asked as we left the wharf and followed the rocky riverbank.

"Harbours Board Maintenance," Danny answered laconically.

We crossed the Flats, a loose collection of peeling tarpaper shacks sprouting flimsy porches and other random add-ons. As we neared the end of this sorry-looking hamlet a shrill voice called out: "Danny!" Turning, I saw a woman with Indian features, probably in her early thirties, on the doorstep of one of the better-looking shanties. But for the hardened lines of her jaw, she would have been quite pretty. She smiled at me faintly and beckoned to Danny. He hung his head, told me he would be back in a minute and strode over to her. While they were exchanging words that I couldn't make out I watched the dredge in the middle of the river. It was scraping up rocks from the bottom in slow, deliberate movements like a boxer slugging at a giant he would never fell.

"That was my aunt," Danny lied when he came back. "She wants me to buy some meat for her."

"What language were you speaking?"

"French." He lowered his eyes, as if fearing a rebuke.

"French!" I marvelled and told him I'd spent my preschool mornings glued to "Chez Hélène". TV was still a year away in Churchill so he'd never heard of it. But the idea of someone being fascinated by the language he spoke at home intrigued him.

"Hey, what's that awful smell?" I asked as we sauntered on. We were coming to a cluster of sheds surrounding an unpainted two-storey structure. I could hear a chugging sound from the interior. Steam rose in puffs from the chimney. Workers, a mix of whites and natives, bustled about the area. Boats were tied up at the nearby pier with others overturned on the ground. As we approached the stench quickly grew unbearable, worse than an outhouse in ninety-degree weather. I pinched my nostrils in disgust.

"It's the whale plant," Danny explained. "I have to go there."

"I'll wait here," I said, turning to face upwind. I sat down on the bank. The river was wide here, wider than at its mouth and far wider than the muddy, slow-moving waterways I'd seen in the south. I felt a bit uneasy as I remembered Mom's warning, for I could sense the powerful pull of the current beneath the rippling surface. It was like sitting alongside a sleeping, primeval beast that I knew could devour me in one gulp should it ever wake up. To quell my anxiety, I tried to concentrate on the dredge as it went through its perfunctory motions, extending the scoop forward over the water, lowering it to the bottom, bringing it up laden with rocks, swivelling to drop them into the hopper with a grating rumble, then swivelling back to repeat the process over and over again. The movement relaxed me but the aura of the river was overpowering. I closed my eyes to imagine the jagged procession of granite creeping inexorably along the riverbed with the current. There are things one can divine at any age and it will dawn on me as I write this, many years from now, that what I grasped instinctively in that moment, besides the Sisyphean nature of the dredge's task, was the bigger picture the procession represented. It had to do with the march of time, which isn't a march at all but a passage, like the riverbed, through which all things proceed to their final end.

My reverie was broken by the drone of an outboard motor growing louder. I couldn't see where it was coming from at first, but then the boat appeared from behind the dredge and veered in my direction, trailing a white mass in its wake. The two men aboard wore oilskins. While the one in the stern reduced the throttle, his companion in the bow stood up with a rope in his hand, preparing to dock a short distance upriver. It was then I realized that the boat was heading for the whale plant and that the white mass bobbing in its wake had a large tailfin. A beluga! A minute later Danny returned with a newsprint package. He unfolded it, revealing two dark red slabs which he displayed with evident satisfaction.

"Yuck! You mean you eat whale meat?" I backed away, curling my lip in scorn.

Danny was crestfallen. "It's for my aunt," he lied again. His hurt expression dismayed me. All of a sudden I was aware of my squeamishness, like when Dad eyed me while savouring the gizzard of a chicken on Sundays. I mustn't be branded a ninny.

Breathing through my mouth, I turned to watch the beluga being fitted with chains and hauled up a ramp onto the pier. I asked Danny to tell me more about the whale hunt. He hesitated, unsure if my interest was genuine, but with a bit more coaxing he related how the animals were harpooned from boats in the estuary, followed to where they surfaced for air and finished off with a rifle before being towed to the plant.

"How do they follow the whales for the kill?"

"The harpoon has a line with a floater attached." He went on to describe how the skin was stripped off and used to make sled harnesses. The blubber was boiled down for the oil (the chugging sound I could hear). Most of the meat, he said, was ground up and sold as feed to fur farms while the choicest flesh was cut up into steaks. I listened dispassionately as the beluga was dragged from the pier towards the awaiting arsenal of blades, grinders and tanks.

An ignominious end for a noble creature? Hardly, as far as I was concerned. Like most people, I thought of whales as big fish and, as it turned out, smellier to boot. Who could have guessed how that perception would be turned on its head just a few years hence, when Greenpeace would be founded in Vancouver? Or how, for that matter, veganism and anti-speciesism will sweep the country one day? Commercial whaling was doomed, and for Churchill, its demise would mark a turning point. The town was unwittingly poised for a remarkable makeover into a beacon for ecotourists, who will flock here in the coming decades to observe the polar bears, belugas and northern lights. The purest of them will view the past butchery of whales as a crime that went unpunished. Which will make Dad a criminal, because unknown to us now he will play a part in the slaughter.

The moral, perhaps, is that it's best not to know what the future holds in store. The dream I had that night portended as much. I was back on the train that brought us north. The scene was deceivingly real at first, a replay of the morning after we left home. I was standing in the corridor outside our sleeping compartment, my face pressed against the window. Mom, Dave and Beth were still asleep in their bunks. Dad wasn't with us. It was early and I'd got up to have a pee. I'd been afraid to step on the pedal that flushed the toilet. I didn't want to hear the racket of the wheels as we sped along the jointed track, or see the blur of ties racing by beneath the drainpipe. But I'd had to look down through the hole in case there was someone waiting to reach up and grab me. At eleven, alone I could still be afraid of the bogeyman. *Clickety-clack. Clickety-clack.* The joins of the track sent up a syncopated rhythm, like rapping on the rim of a snare drum, with the stress falling on the fourth and final beat. This was followed a fraction of a second later by the same sound but fainter, like an echo, as the rear wheels of the car slid over the same join. I wanted to count how many bars of this clickety-clack made a mile, starting from a milepost, but it was a hopeless task:

by the time I got to thirty or forty I couldn't remember how many tens I'd already counted with my fingers. I could feel myself becoming hypnotized by the sound and by the numbingly repetitive scenery that swept by the window. Mile 255, long stand of pines, bend, blasted rock... Mile 256, long stand of pines, bend, blasted rock... Mile 256, long stand of pines, bend... Wait— Something was wrong! The same milepost started passing by again and again, as if the train was moving in circles. The scene changed and suddenly I found myself riding outside the sleeping car in the open air, my arms stretched out on either side to hold onto the car behind me and the one in front. Then the cars morphed into the twins, Terry and Jake, my bosom buddies in Norton. We were holding hands while dancing in a circle at our family's farewell party. The whole little town was gathered in the community hall. The clickety-clack of the train wheels melted into a jig that went around and round like the dancers. But every so often, at a signal from the fiddler, we had to break the circle and form a line. This always happened when I found myself at the spot where the break had to come. I kept losing the partner behind me. And then I was on the railway line to Churchill again, riding out in the open, hanging onto the car ahead of me. I looked back and saw empty track.

The vision popped as I awoke, troubled. Dave was sleeping soundly in the upper bunk. Sandy, our tawny cat, was curled up beside my pillow. I stroked his back lightly, thankful that he had remained part of our life. Sandy stretched his front paws contentedly and laid his head sideways, his eyes shut tight. Little do we know now but he will be the one left behind when we depart from Churchill in three years' time. He will turn into a prowler, wandering off for days, sleeping in the crawl spaces under other houses. And little do I know now but the dream was a premonition of my own life to come, a trail of broken circles.

School started a few days later. By then I'd met Jeff and Robin, both a year ahead of me in school. Both had moreover lived a full year in Churchill and knew the score. Robin had spent the summer visiting relatives in southwestern Ontario and Jeff was jealous as his own ragged family had only gone to Flin Flon. To save face he raved about the fishing there, bragging that he'd caught several large pike and a lake trout. I asked them what they thought of Danny.

"His mother's a squaw," Jeff scoffed.

"My mom says she's a fallen woman," added Robin, who enjoyed quoting his mother. Neither Jeff nor I knew exactly what this meant but it sounded disastrous. Jeff giggled. I looked down at my feet.

There are thirteen of us in our combined fifth and sixth-grade class: six boys and seven girls including Moses and Janie, the two Chipewyan children at the back. They're mostly ignored by everyone except Cynthia, who is friendly with Janie and censures the other girls when they tease her about her clothes or unwashed hair. Moses doesn't have anyone to defend him but me, although discouraging Jeff and Robin from poking fun at him, I don't consider him a friend. The problem with Moses is not only his extreme shyness, which is often misconstrued as disinterest, but also his difficulty with English. Assuming this to be an unsurmountable hurdle, Miss Sadler asks Janie to interpret for her and gives him third-grade readers and colouring books to keep him occupied during geography and science periods. He and Janie congregate with the other Chipewyan kids at recess, ostracized as much by the Cree and Métis as by us whites. They go to the Anglican Church at noon for a lunch of soup, milk and sandwiches that Beth and I help Mom make once a week, with tinned salmon and peanut butter. The rest of us go home for lunch, which usually consists of the same fare.

We begin each school day by standing to sing "O Canada" and say the Lord's Prayer, heads bowed, hands clasped behind our backs or folded over our private parts. I know when Jeff, just ahead of me, is scratching his scrotum because Sandra, across from him in the girls' row, rolls her eyes and looks away. After the prayer we sit down and listen, again with bowed heads, while Miss Sadler reads from the Bible.

For a time traveller from the twenty-first century, these rituals would smack of regimentation and bigotry. But again, that reflects how much attitudes will have changed. Personally, I find our rendition of the national anthem embarrassing: half the class is tone-deaf and Astrid screeches the last line like a demented magpie. We sang a lot better in Norton. Yet the irony is greater, for our listless performance belies a budding nationalism—a kind of springtime in the air that we are oblivious to but which a visitor from the future couldn't help but note. There is an earnest search for a Canadian identity in this period. The country is proud of its new prime minister, Lester Pearson, who won the Nobel Peace Prize and whose government, with hard prodding from the left, will introduce state pensions, student loans, universal health care (Americans, take note!) and the modern flag. Global hegemony in hockey will have to wait until the issue of amateurs and professionals is resolved.

As for the bible thumping, the agnostics and other fringe groups who might object to it know their place. And those of our parents who don't drag us to church probably say to themselves that a bit of religion will do us good. But, like a little knowledge, in our case, a little religion will turn out to be a dangerous thing. One reason has to do with Miss Sadler. This is her first teaching job and she's taking the role of educating us to heart. However, there's more to her zeal than greenhorn altruism: she also aims to make a good impression so she can secure the needed references, leave this dump and move back to civilization. The result is an overbearing, overblown style that rubs many of us the wrong way, especially the boys. When it comes to giving voice to the Scriptures, she loves to read with fervour and declaims the sumptuous Hebrew names pompously. Robin, whose mother teaches Sunday school, is embarrassed. Danny squirms. Jeff snorts under his breath while Roger, the other white boy, would love to mimic him but can't because he is too close to the front. Personally, I find Miss Sadler's gusto amusing, like bad acting, but to me the Old Testament stories, borne by the rhythms of Elizabethan English, transcend such mannerisms. Their exotic settings and larger-than-life characters enchant me and it's in this dreamy state that I often look sideways at Cynthia, further mesmerized by her blond hair and sculpted features. In later life, I'll wonder if I've ever re-experienced such a perfect union of body and mind. Last week during Bible reading, she turned and caught me staring at her. I blushed, which made her giggle.

"Cynthia," Miss Sadler chided her gently. She is always lenient with the girls, who are suck-ups for the most part. My face burned hotter. I closed my eyes and struggled to rebuild my cocoon. Later, as we were fishing our math books out of the drawers under our seats, a voice hissed my name. I looked up to see Cynthia scrunching up her delectable nose and sticking her tongue out at me.

Miss Sadler doesn't read the Bible *in extenso* but in long excerpts that dispense with some of the less important episodes while preserving the narrative. Thus, by the time Dad nabs Moses at The Bay (the Hudson's Bay Company general store) we've finished Genesis and are launching into Exodus. Now, as some of us know, the editing of the Good Book had a second, ulterior motive: it's also intended to weed out earthier details, such as "And he went in unto her and knew her ...", lest our inquisitive young minds put two and two together. I will guess in later years that the censor (doubtless some dour, pudgy-faced pastor) could never have imagined us twisting the passages he left intact. The upshot is that, between his dearth of street wisdom and Miss Sadler's bombastic rendering, we are on a collision course. It all starts quite innocently when the name Moses first comes up. We've heard it before, most of us in church, but the presence of our bashful companion at the back of the class creates a kind of wacky time warp that has the girls clamping their hands over their mouths to cover their chortling. Heads turn for a glimpse of our own Moses, as we picture him coming to the rescue of the priest's seven daughters and watering their flock. There are even some outright guffaws at the idea of the priest "giving" one of these maidens to the young Moses, like a birthday present, to be his bride. Miss Sadler pronounces her name, Zip-po-rah, with unusual relish, making the clash of times and cultures more outlandish still.

"Class!" Miss Sadler raises her voice, unable to berate any of us individually because one of the louder guffaws has come from Wendy, her prissy pet up front. We all strive to stifle our laughter. "This is Not a comedy!" Miss Sadler shrills, straining to keep her composure.

The next day is far worse. To begin with, Robin and I are already hyped up in the schoolyard after listening to Max Ferguson on the radio at breakfast. In one of his zanier live-to-air broadcasts, he sawed, hammered and wired together a rocket which he announced he was about to fly to the moon. He added a front porch as the final feature before blasting off at the end of the program, with his "Sooo looooong!" trailing off into the theme music. Space flight is all the rage these days and the Ruskies have got ahead in the race again by launching the first woman cosmonaut into orbit. Thus, we're jabbering excitedly along with Jeff, Roger and Danny when Miss Spencer, one of the secondary teachers in the main school building, comes out to ring the bell. We form an unruly line at the door of our trailer, boisterously poking and slapping at each other as we troop inside to take off our coats.

When it comes time for Bible reading, we're still bubbling over and our excitement has spread to the girls, who are also a bit unhinged from yesterday. What's more, Jeff and Roger start snorting in turns as the story of Moses moves on to the burning bush. Roger, who is more than a year older than any of us (he's repeating grade six), already has a monstrous growth of pubic hair. He proudly showed it off to Jeff a couple of Saturdays ago while they leafed through a dog-eared copy of *Playboy,* he'd found in his dad's hunting bag. Miss Sadler doesn't notice the smirks at first but Yana and Carla, the two hussies in the girls' row, catch on as the word "bush" keeps coming up. Soon they're exchanging knowing smiles with Jeff and Danny, who is pretending to slap out a fire in his lap. Even the other girls seem to end up getting the joke—all except Wendy, of course, who looks around helplessly. Miss Sadler, no longer able to ignore the conspiratorial glances and muffled snickering but intent on keeping order, reads on louder to show her annoyance:

"And the Lord said unto him, what is that in thine hand? And he said, A rod."

Here half the class explodes, including to my great dismay Cynthia, who holds her jiggling sides to contain her laughter. But it's no use: the spasms become uncontrollable when she sees that I'm red as a beet. She points at me, to the delight of the sucks and our Chipewyan classmates, who in the meantime have figured out what a rod is. There's no stopping us now. If the puritanical pastor could only see us, he'd be gaping in disbelief!

Miss Sadler glowers at us. "You are IN-SUF-FER-ABLE!" she bellows finally, slamming the bible shut. We've already started wiping our eyes, bracing for her to harangue us some more and sober us up with the prospect of lines to write over the weekend. But before she can open her mouth again Danny, who has no doubt been restraining himself with untold effort, lets out a resounding fart—a long trombone blast timed perfectly to hammer her interjection home like a crescendo. All hell breaks loose! We hold our noses with one hand and slap our thighs with the other, roaring with laughter. Danny, abandoning all pretence of contrition, joins in. Miss Sadler bursts into tears. Yanking open the top drawer of her desk, she hauls out the strap: a wide, 18-inch band of stiff black leather that is dreaded and seldom seen. Wielding it like a whip, she marches down the aisle between the boys' row and the cupboards along the wall and delivers a well-aimed whack on the shoulder to each of us. Robin, being in front, gets the first one. He winces but keeps silent (his dad would be proud). Roger's wallop comes next and then Jeff's. He makes the mistake of covering his shoulder with his left hand and takes it flat across the knuckles, causing him to yelp in pain. I'm next. I cringe but the blow scarcely stings because of the fury Miss Sadler is saving for Danny. She belts him five times brutally, then hovers over him, shaking and livid, hands on her narrow hips.

"I'll teach you some manners!" she snarls between gritted teeth. Danny hangs his head sullenly. "Now wipe those smirks off your faces and take out your math books!" she barks at the rest of us. I'll say this much: she didn't touch Moses. Whether because she'd already vented her rage on Danny, or because she knew Moses was innocent, I'm not sure. Perhaps we've misjudged her. Some years from now, in high school, I'll try to picture Miss Sad Face on the jury in *To Kill a Mockingbird*. Would she be capable of dissenting? When we come back inside the trailer after recess, she looks drained and irritable. The list of homework is already posted on the blackboard. It begins with *Write 100 X I promise to be quiet and respectful during Bible reading.*

I wake up the next morning with a vision of the flailing strap coming closer and closer. But then I remember it's Saturday and the scene evaporates. Pulling my clothes on quietly so as not to disturb Dave, I get up and go to the back of the house to relieve myself, holding my nose and shivering over the oval hole in the bench. In the kitchen I splash cold water on my hands, rub the soap a bit, while leaving it in the dish, and slide two fingers over each cheek in case Mom sniffs them. She has already made porridge and left it on the stove. Taking a bowl from the cupboard, I scrape some out of the pot and sit down at the table. The door to the back porch opens and closes quietly. That will be Mom, who scolds us for banging it.

"You're up early," she greets me in surprise as she comes in with an armful of laundry. Usually, I sleep in until ten on Saturdays. I pour milk and brown sugar on my porridge to cool it down. "Did you make your bed? Remember, you have to clean up your room today."

"Dave's still sleeping. But I'll do everything when he gets up," I assure her, proffering a cheek as she bends down to give me a peck on the forehead. Unlike me she invariably smells good and her light brown curls are always neatly brushed. Although she doesn't flaunt them, she must be aware of her good looks, which clash with her humble Interlake origins and the rough-edged towns she and Dad have called home. Instead of kissing my cheek she cups my chin in her hand, turns my head from side to side and inspects my face.

"My, aren't we clever," she mocks me. "Now march over to the sink and wash properly!"

I obey without protest because on Saturdays I receive my allowance and today I can't chance being docked. The fifty cents will just cover my admission to the afternoon movie, plus a bar of toffee and a new comic book at S&M's. But before the film I have an appointment with Danny to visit a kennel on the outskirts of town. Danny loves dogs and recently confided to me that he will raise sled dogs when he grows up. I told him that was dumb because, by then, everyone who needs to travel around the countryside in winter will own a snowmobile.

"You never lived in the bush," he scoffed. "Whaddya do when they break down or you run outta gas fifty miles from town?"

I said there would be a solution. My faith in progress is invincible.

We meet after lunch. The kennel smells a bit less evil than the whale plant so this time I stay with Danny to get a good look. Actually "kennel" is a grand name for what it is: a chicken-wire enclosure held together with a two-by-four frame. Jeremy, the man who owns the place, works for the CNR and is breeding dogs as a hobby. The breeding stock are a pair of pure Canadian Eskimo Dogs acquired from a trapper who still uses a sled. The couple have had a litter of five pups, their mottled coats ranging from mainly white to mainly black. They have mask-like faces with brown or amber eyes and are very vocal, barking in a frantic, unbroken chorus as if they don't know how to stop. The yapping rises to a fever pitch when Jeremy enters the cage, collars a pup that is cuddled next to the mother and brings it out, cursing the other dogs and shooing them away from the door as he steps out. He holds the writhing animal forward in both hands to avoid the pee that's squirting from its trembling pink and black underbelly. It yelps in bewilderment.

"This is Nicky," Danny tells me proudly, taking the pup and stroking it while keeping its limbs still in an arm-lock. I notice that it doesn't try to lick his face like most young dogs do. It appears to be only a few weeks old but is already quite strong. "He's gonna be mine if I can talk Mom into it." Nicky shivers and jerks his head back and forth in excitement, seized every few seconds by a new fit of yelping. I pat him and listen while Danny and Jeremy talk. It turns out they have a deal. To pay for Nicky, Danny is providing Jeremy with fish as dog food: ciscoes he catches in a net by the shore of the bay. He has them frozen at the whale plant to kill the worms, he explains to me later as we walk back into town. He keeps the whitefish and occasional Arctic char for his mother and himself and for a friend of hers who supplies the net.

"When do you check it?" I ask, seeing a new opportunity for adventure.

"I go a couple of times a week. I'd check it more often but Mom says it keeps me from schoolwork."

"What's so special about Nicky?"

"He's got a hip problem. It's not serious but nobody'll buy him. Jeremy was gonna drown him in the river so I wanted to save him."

"Doesn't sound like much of a deal to me," I say and am immediately ashamed of my callousness. Danny is silent. "What if your mom says no?"

"Then he's saved for a while at least."

I still ponder this as we arrive back in the main street, a wide band of sandy dirt ending in a square with a flagpole flanked by rusty cannons and a circle of white-painted rocks that I will stumble over in winter. There is no multiplex yet, (it will come in a decade), so the town's centre of gravity is this empty space bordered by the railway station and hotels to our left, the green and white Hudson's Bay store-cum-trading post opposite, the federal building, RCMP barracks and Catholic church to our right, and behind where we're standing the Igloo Theatre—a rundown structure covered with peeling, pale blue paint. Roughly twice the size of our house, it is advertised by a sign depicting a polar bear nosing an igloo, as if it were wondering what might be inside. Danny is expansive for once.

"I'm gonna build a sled for Nicky to pull and hunt rabbits on weekends," he enthuses. "Mom knows another guy who has a camp upriver. He promised to lend me his .22."

"I thought you had to be twelve to hunt."

"Mom can sign for me. She'll say we need the food. In any case I'll be twelve next year."

I look at him with new respect. Here's a kid my age who already has plans, like a grown-up, and is capable of bringing home meat and fish year round. All I can do is clean my room for fifty cents a week. Even Dave, five years older than me, is just starting to earn some money of his own by stocking shelves and delivering flyers for The Bay. Danny wants to be independent—an entrepreneur.

At the end of the street people get on the bus to Fort Churchill, the military base six miles east. The Fort, as we call it, comprises half a dozen clusters of identical two-storey apartment blocks which are laid out in neat rows and connected by roofed corridors. The clusters are in turn arranged like satellites around a handful of large buildings that include a commissary, the school that Dave attends, an indoor skating rink, a bowling alley and a proper movie theatre. It's a far more respectable community than the slummy harbour town of Churchill. A lot of Air Force people live there, along with scientists working on the Black Brant rockets program and they look down on our lot as riff-raff. On his last visit to the Fort, to see a hockey game, Danny was beaten up and swore he would never go back.

"Buncha pricks!" he spits on the ground, remembering how they kicked him while he was down and left him in a crumpled heap. He nods to the passers-by, telling me who they are once they're out of earshot: a fireman, two railroad crewmen in overalls and the manager of one of the hotels. Everyone recognizes Danny but only the hotel manager says hello between puffs on his cigar. Teenagers are starting to congregate in front of The Bay, opposite us, occasionally looking our way. Beth isn't among them and I remember that she's babysitting. Danny says the group will probably be coming to the movie and points out the toughs I should steer clear of. While we stand waiting for the theatre to open, Jeff and Robin amble up. They both look miffed. I didn't tell them Danny would be joining us. Jeff, still sore about the strap, immediately tears into him.

"There's the jerk who can't keep a lid on his asshole," he growls. I'm about to come to Danny's defence but he gestures to me to stay out of it. Putting on the deadpan expression he uses to counter hostility, he keeps his voice level.

"You can't help body functions." His equanimity surprises me and makes the janitor's son look shabby.

"Bodily functions," Robin corrects him, trumping them

both. But Jeff won't be deterred.

"Well, I don't wanna sit with anyone who's gonna stink up the place," he continues, his jaw thrust forward. I can see the clod is itching for a shoving match or more. To cool him down I suggest we sit in pairs on opposite sides of the aisle. Jeff scowls but Robin pokes him in the ribs until he nods assent.

The teenagers have crossed the street and joined the youngsters forming a haphazard line in front of the theatre. Three mothers with young urchins in tow keep a semblance of order. I tense up as Cynthia approaches with Wendy, both tossing their freshly washed hair. Will they ask us to save them seats? My heart starts racing. But then it lurches and sinks—they stop alongside the group of seventh-graders and turn their backs to us. Jeff utters an obscenity and bites his lip. Then he winks at Robin: something is up. Meanwhile, Danny and I have managed to hold our position and are still in front of the door when it finally opens from inside. Blotto Balanchuck, the proprietor, hangs his jaw and looks down the queue with a sour face, counting. He makes us wait while he takes his place in the plywood booth at the entrance.

"Gonna behave today?" He hisses at me, looking up with bloodshot eyes over his black-rimmed glasses.

"Yes sir," I reply meekly. He bawled me out the last time for breaking my toffee on the armrest of my seat and made me sit at the back as punishment. Now, however, the quarter I lay on the counter mollifies him. He drops it into his cash box and tears a blue ticket off the roll. After Danny pays, we push through the curtain into the dingy projection hall. There are a dozen rows of beaten-up wooden seats divided by a narrow aisle. We go straight to the middle. The front rows fill up with younger kids mostly, so I'm surprised when Wendy and Cynthia claim the seats immediately in front of Danny and me. They remain standing, still ignoring us studiously, and my heart sinks even deeper into my gut when I realize they're saving the rest of the row for the grade-seven boys they were bantering with outside. Jeff and Robin, who hung back and watched us all choose our places, seat themselves across the aisle a row back from Danny and me.

The movie we've come to see is *The Three Stooges Meet Hercules*, billed as 'More Fun Than a Roman Circus' and 'The Entertainment Event of a Lifetime!' This second pitch is on the level where the Churchill crowd is concerned, for we are rubes to the core. When the lights go out, the general chatter rises to a tidal wave of cheers, clapping, foot stomping and ear-piercing whistles that drown out the crackle of the speakers and the whir and rattle of the projector at the back. Beside me in the aisle seat, Danny watches the screen avidly as it lights up with the kick-off Woody Woodpecker cartoon. It's clear he doesn't go to the movies often. I sit in sullen silence, still burning with humiliation at the girls' standoffishness. I would be spared the pain of seeing Cynthia's face, hidden by her tumble of hair, were it not for Wendy in front of me, who keeps poking her and the boy on her right in great excitement to get their attention. She's obviously keen on this Brylcreemed dandy, named Lennie. I've seen him talking her up in the schoolyard. How can love be such an easy game for some?

Concerned at least to get my money's worth, I try to concentrate on the cartoon instead. The plot is coming to a head, with Woody thinking he's having a bath while in fact he's being slow-boiled by Greedy Gabby Gator. All of a sudden, Danny jerks and lifts a hand to rub the back of his head.

"What's the matter?" I ask. He rounds on the teenagers behind us but they don't take any notice and go on jabbering excitedly, about the Buick Skylark the garage mechanic recently brought up by train from Thompson.

"I dunno, something hit me."

"Maybe somebody threw it," I offer, unconvinced by my own suggestion. I glance across the aisle at Jeff and Robin, who sit stock-still, eyes forward. Even less convincing. "It's them," I say to Danny. "I'll bet they've got a peashooter."

The full story will come out from Robin on Monday after school. He has contributed the large plastic straw from a milkshake his father bought him at the Hudson Hotel while Jeff has brought a pocketful of the dried peas his mother uses to make soup. They're hard enough to sting, as we know from our war games, where Jeff whips out his spring-loaded pea gun whenever he's cornered. He likes to torment Sandy with it too. Delivered from a peashooter with the right-sized straw and a strong blast of air, the peas travel farther and smart when they hit bare skin. Jeff's first shot was at Danny as payback for the strap, but with Robin's prompting they step up their mischief, rolling with the action of the Three Stooges film. Here's a recap:

The villain, Dimsal, pulls up in front of his drugstore with the girl, Diane, in his convertible. Dimsal wants Diane to warm up to him and dump her milquetoast inventor boyfriend, Schuyler. Robin points to a grade-three boy two rows ahead whose drunkard father badmouths the Mounties. Jeff looks around to make sure nobody's watching, looses a pea that hits home behind the little wretch's ear and quickly stows the straw in his jacket pocket. The kid tries to challenge the bigger boys behind him but they tell him to shut up. Jeff and Robin hug each other in glee.

A few minutes later, sparks from Schuyler's overheating time machine ignite sky-rockets that fly in all directions. Jeff takes advantage of the general excitement to aim and shoot a fourth-grader three rows ahead. There's a commotion, with accusations flying like the rockets, but again the others couldn't care less as the time machine, a B-movie contraption with rows of buttons and dials down the front and a flashing light on top, takes off with the Stooges, Schuyler and Diane on board.

Seeing he can get away with murder, Jeff goes after bigger game. Actually, he and Robin planned to get even with Wendy today on a number of scores. Besides being chief tattletale and suck of our class, she infuriated Robin last week by solving a math problem that had left him stumped. As for Jeff, he has a secret crush on her and knows it will never lead anywhere because his father is a janitor. Like me eating my heart out over Cynthia, he's stewing at the spectacle of Wendy flirting with Brylcreem Lennie and today's cold shoulder has galvanized his spite. But on Robin's advice he bides his time until he can strike with calculation.

The Stooges, Schuyler and Diane are being feted at the palace of the tyrant Odius for unwittingly helping him defeat Ulysses, who is being held downstairs in the dungeon. When the learned Schuyler tells the Stooges that Ulysses should have won the battle, to set history straight they go down to free him. When they pound on the bottom of a bar of his cell to drive it upwards, it breaks through the floor above and through the table where Hercules, in Odius' employ, is cracking nuts with his biceps. The bar pokes him in the eye. He rams it back down on the Stooges' toes. Danny, I and the rest of the audience howl with delight as the bar keeps going up and down and Hercules fumes. Amid the merriment, Jeff points the straw carefully and hits Wendy, who is bent forward hooting with laughter, midships between the shoulders. She winces and wheels on me, her green eyes flashing in the dim light. "Was that you?"

"No", I say, "it was probably Jeff and Robin." She looks across and sees them grinning nonchalantly. They even wave at her, the cheeky buggers. I can feel her eyes drilling into me. "I don't care who it was," she hisses, "But if any of you tries it again, I'll get Lennie and his buddies to beat your brains out after the show! If you have any!" I make a helpless gesture with my hands.

Not long after, the audience is going wild again as the Stooges, who have escaped Hercules and taken refuge in the ladies' bath disguised as handmaids, are unmasked and run about in accelerated vaudeville mayhem. Jeff, intent on setting Wendy on fire again, draws a new bead on her. But Danny, who has been watching out of the corner of his eagle eye, thrusts up his hand as Jeff lets fly and the pea is deflected onto the sleeve of Cynthia's sky-blue sweater. She brushes it off without flinching. Danny and I leer at Jeff and Robin, pulling the corners of our mouths into wide grins with our forefingers. They pout like kids who've been refused candy.

They don't try anything again for a while, waiting for Danny to let his guard down. The chance comes when the Stooges are trying to play it wise by backing away from Odius, whom they expect to open a trap door, only to fall into the one he's opened behind them. Danny, unable or unwilling to understand that it's just a goofy comedy, can't watch the scene. He looks down as the Stooges pick themselves up in the dungeon below and covers his eyes when a caged lion appears out of nowhere and roars into the eye of the camera (a cheap insert from another film, I'll read many years from now). Jeff, who may have been distracted by the unseemly lion, misses his shot. The pea whistles by Wendy's glossy red mane and smacks Lennie on the cheek. He jumps up and whirls around, ready to lay into me as the closest accomplice. I protest but he sticks a finger into my collarbone. "Take that thing away from him," he glowers, "or else!" Deciding that things have gone too far, I start pushing past Danny under Cynthia's approving gaze. But there's no need: Blotto Balanchuck is already striding down the aisle like the town marshal, his mouth set in a grim line. He grabs Jeff by the scruff of the neck and Robin by the arm and marches them up the aisle to the exit. Jeff gets a kick in the ass while Blotto warns Robin he'll tell his father if there's a next time.

The film ends well, not only because Schuyler gets his girl back from the lecherous Odius but also because, having become a muscleman and made Hercules say uncle in the meantime, he has the gumption to stand up to the drugstore owner Dimsal when they get back to their 1960s Ithica in New York state. As for Odius- (who looks a lot like Dimsal), they cut him loose from the time machine on the way home. He falls to the ground on the American frontier, sometime in the mid-1800s, and is chased off the screen by a horde by whooping Indians (another cheap insert). I feel vindicated by Schuyler's story, having stood up – literally – in the Igloo Theatre to take up the cudgels for our female classmates. They will never thank me, of course, but I like to think there's a trace of an appreciative smile on Cynthia's face when they put on their coats to leave.

"Why were you afraid of that corny lion?" I ask Danny as we prepare to follow them out.

"I dunno. I just didn't like the way they got trapped."

Back home I start my lines for Monday, dividing them up into three segments (I promise to be / quiet and respectful / during Bible reading) so the monotony won't make my mind wander. Miss Sadler warned us that she won't accept any crossed-out words or blotches. I want to do at least half the lines today because tomorrow after breakfast we're invited to ride the tugboat with Dad to meet one of the last ships waiting to come into port. They need a pilot to steer them through the dredged channel. It's the first week of October and the shipping season is ending.[1]

The next morning breaks grey and chilly. Mom carries a basket containing a picnic and a thermos of tea while Dad brings a plastic tarp to protect us from the spray. This being Sunday, the harbour is quiet as we file over the gangplank onto the ageing tug, its faded black and red hull partly hidden by a row of tires that serve as shock absorbers along the waterline. I'm the last to cross after Dad, Mom and Beth (Dave has stayed home to work on a science project). The cramped deck is already swaying. I grit my teeth, knowing it's too late to back out.

The pilot comes on board a minute later, greeting each of us gregariously and pumping our hands. Soon he falls into conversation with Dad and the captain in the tiny cabin. He seems a capable fellow—tall, bearded, dashing. This posting in the north is temporary, I hear him say. Indeed, he looks too worldly to have grown up in Churchill. No one I know has roots here except Danny, Moses, Janie and Cynthia (who was brought by her parents at the age of two). I ask Mom why he's called a pilot.

---

[1] This is long before any evidence of global warming. Doomsayers are instead speculating about a new Ice Age. An article in our supplemental reading book concludes with an advisory (I swear this is true!) that the US should start preparing for an influx of Canadian climate refugees. Fifty-some years on, the talk will be equally dire with warnings that the boreal forest will one day follow the Arctic ice pack into oblivion. In the meantime, the port of Churchill will see its shipping season steadily lengthen until its shutdown, for commercial reasons, in 2016.

Pilots fly airplanes. She tells me there are river pilots too, but I wonder why there isn't a separate word. Polysemy confuses me, like homonyms, and despite being an avid reader I'm often challenged by English spelling.

We cast off, swing around and head towards the mouth of the river. The captain opens the throttle in midstream and the tug heaves as we plough hard into the swells. I feel queasy. Mom unfolds the tarpaulin and spreads it around us. We pass a buoy, resembling a top hollowed out at the tip with a bell inside. The flashing light reminds me of the time machine in the Stooges film.

"Why do they call it a boy?" I ask Beth, huddled beside me. She's three years older than me and considerably more focused.

"Buoys are buoyant," she tells me. "They float. You can call it a channel marker if you like."

"That's clearer," I reply gloomily, starting to feel seasick.

We're midway between Cape Merry (which for many years I will think is Cape Mary) and Fort Prince of Wales (which I will assume to be Fort Prince of Whales until I see the name carved on the stone gate next summer, wondering why the 'h' is missing). It's here, at the midpoint in the mouth of the river, that the fortifications' designers planned to catch invaders in a crossfire between the fort and the battery. Yet little history was ever written in this God-forsaken place. The only time Fort Price of Wales was attacked, by three French warships in 1782, the forty-odd Hudson's Bay Company employees infamously surrendered without firing a shot. The French destroyed part of the fort but it was all in vain: when the belligerents ended their costly war the next year (after dragging in Spain, the Netherlands and the newly founded United States, not to mention all their colonies, from the Caribbean to Gibraltar and from India to

Africa), the Hudson Bay trading posts were returned to the British and settled back into quiet decline. Fort Prince of Wales was rebuilt as a historical monument after the railroad came, in the late 1920s. More compelling, when I see it a couple of years from now, is the inscription that Samuel Hearne, the man who surrendered to the French, etched on a nearby rock in 1767, when he set out to find the fabled Coppermine River.

By now we're out on the open bay and approaching the *Pstrowski*, a decrepit Polish freighter. A crewman is already uncoiling a rope ladder and lowering it down the side for the pilot. I look back over the tug's foaming wake. Churchill, already a low-slung town close up, from this distance appears flattened and forlorn. The grain elevators are the only structure whose lines suggest a vanishing point beyond the chaotic band of windswept rocks, strewn like rueful remnants of a rebellion crushed eons ago by the leaden sky. The sensation of floating in a wayward time capsule assails me. I feel faint. A mass rises in my stomach and I lurch towards the railing. Beth grabs my arm.

"Ben, what's wrong?" From the stricken look on her face I must be white, green or some other ghastly colour.

"I'm gonna... be sick," I gasp through the welling vomit. She holds my arm firmly while I retch over the side of the tug. My head is swimming. The smell of oil makes it spin faster. No longer able to stand, I slump down on all fours and then lie flat, sticking my head out over the edge, puking my guts out on the tires below. A wave of fatigue descends on me and clamps me to the deck. I'm sweating profusely. The chill wind and spray whip my face. Beth tries to pull me up but I shake her off. I'm miserable and want nothing, no one. As we slow and manoeuvre alongside the *Pstrowski*, the tug stops heaving and starts bobbing up and down, its engine idling. My nausea is worse than ever.

Between empty belches I try to fix my blinking gaze on a point in the water. An iridescent film of oil is forming on the swells. Mercifully, the fatigue envelops me like a heavy cloak and I probably sleep for a minute. I feel myself falling, slipping headlong without a ripple beneath the pearly surface, somersaulting ever so gently. The throb of the tug's engine becomes muffled and a grey-green world gathers me into its cold bosom. The stillness is soothing. I'm intrigued, but not afraid, when hairs tickle my arm. Inspecting the thing clutching at my elbow, I see it's a worm with several pairs of legs and what might be its head at the opposite end. I brush it off and continue my slow descent, mesmerized by a gaggle of jellyfish resembling Christmas ornaments hung on an invisible bough. Eager to discover more denizens of this bizarre wonder world, I scan the murky depths and spot a second group of jellies, comb-shaped, which undulate in a lascivious dance. Like sirens baiting a trap. And then I gape, stupefied. As the outlines of the bottom loom larger, the ghostly shapes crystallize into a gallery of spiny, hard-shelled creatures dotting the bay-bed. My fascination turns to anxiety and then to dread: one of them, lying inert, is mostly a mouth and teeth, with more teeth down its throat, while another waves feathery limbs appended to its misshapen exoskeleton. Still others crawl at a glacial pace over the sand and algae bottom. One of these has at least thirty legs tipped with claws. Another sports tentacles, like a spiny insect; another has rows of spikes, like a stony hedgehog; while still another, curved at both ends, looks like a fork in the evolutionary path from prawns to hairbrushes. I sink to the bottom and lie motionless on my back, staring up at an armoured fish that circles ominously overhead. It has a gaping mouth, wicked teeth and multiple fins protruding from its back and sides. I close my eyes and pray that this is all a dream.

Dad

Churchill, November 1963

"You're kidding."

"No, I'm not and I can show you," Dave says, heading back out of our bedroom. "I know where Mom keeps the string." He's a born teacher and loves demonstrating science concepts, especially to an avid spectator like me. We've just come home from the S&M store and are excited about four large prop planes we saw flying in formation towards the airport three miles away. Dave recognized them as US KC-97 Stratofreighters, aerial tankers whose job it is to refuel B-52 bombers. "They used to be stationed here but now they only come once in a while, for exercises," he told me. After a minute he returns to our room with a ball of white cotton string. Taking the free end in the fingers of his left hand, he goes to the globe on his desk, finds the state of Nebraska, places the end of the string on Lincoln and holds it there with his thumb. "This is their home base," he informs me.

"How do you know that? Shouldn't it be secret?"

"I heard it from a guy at school." He's referring to Fort Churchill School at the military base. "But watch this," he continues. "You turn the globe to the left…" he instructs me, "…Slowly." I do so and he unwinds the string from the ball in his other hand, stretching it across the north-eastern United States, the North Atlantic and Western and Eastern Europe to Moscow.

"Stop!" he orders. "Now mark the distance with my pen." I uncap the cartridge pen on his desk with my free hand and press the nib to the string at the black star dwarfed by the hulking orange mass of the USSR. "Now turn the globe back to where we started and tilt it towards you." I do, and this time he plays out the string north across Canada and the polar ice cap. "Tilt it some more," he directs, struggling to keep the bottom end of the string pinned on Lincoln. The metal shaft and ring protruding from the North Pole forces him east of Moscow but he's made his point: the ink mark on the string he's holding in his right hand is situated much farther south, in Turkey.

"So, it's shorter over Hudson Bay!" I marvel.

"A lot shorter."

I survey the sprawling archipelago between Greenland and Alaska. Three things strike me. First, there isn't a single island that I could have drawn from memory though some are bigger than the Maritime Provinces. Second, the distance to the USSR may well be shorter that way but it still looks incredibly far away. And finally, Churchill, our lonely outpost in what we imagine as the north, is nowhere near the Arctic Circle. The real north seems unbelievably vast and vacant. Does it really belong to us? The Americans claim it doesn't. My mental picture of a giant, imperious B-52 suddenly shrivels.

"There's nothing up there," I conclude. "What if the bombers lose an engine?"

"Well, they've got eight, so even if one or two fail they'll lose some altitude but can keep going indefinitely."

The idea of an engine or two failing near the North Pole leaves a pit in my stomach but I don't say so. I'm still hyped up by this novel perspective and am keen to share it with my friends, along with what I've learned about the tankers. It all smacks of the classified stickers and red-sealed envelopes in Dad's twin-volume *Secrets and Stories of the War*.

The opportunity to break the news comes the next afternoon. It's Saturday and the four of us – Jeff, Robin, Danny and I – are playing in my room. Jeff and Robin grudgingly accepted Danny because I invited him and because we have nowhere else to go: Jeff's place is chock full; Robin's mother would never allow a bunch of rambunctious kids in her apartment; and Danny's shack in the Flats would never do. We're playing war (what else?), which consists of a machine-gun nest under Dave's desk (manned by me), a bunker under my bed (manned by Danny), a grenade launcher on top of my bed (manned by Jeff) and a space station with a flying saucer that glows in the dark on Dave's upper bunk (manned by Robin). Dave is working at the Bay. We've been playing for about an hour when Mom, tired of our yelling and thumping on the walls, shoos us outdoors.

We huddle around the fort we dug in the snowdrift behind my house three weeks ago, after the first winter storm. By now, the wind from the bay has nearly filled it in. What's more, the stockpile of snowballs we made is exhausted and the snow is too hard and dry to make new ones. It's only three o'clock but night is falling fast. Icy air darts inside the hoods of our parkas, nipping at our noses and cheeks. Jeff is pretending to shoot down Messerschmitts with an ack-ack gun. I envy him at times because his father served in the army in Holland and tells real war stories. He brought back souvenirs: a Luger, which Jeff showed to me with considerable pride, and a German helmet that he put on once to come and meet me at the door. I interrupt his antics by dismissing the Messerschmitts as mosquitoes compared with the B-52s flying over the pole towards Russia, part of war games – real war games – taking place this very moment on our doorstep.

To my consternation, the others say nothing and for a second my disappointment turns to alarm. Am I spilling military intelligence? 'Loose lips sink ships,' the warning echoes in my mind. But there's nothing awkward about the others' silence, which Robin soon breaks. He tells us he overheard a conversation between the two junior Mounties about the B-52s' flight path and about Chrome Dome, another US Air Force operation that keeps nuclear-armed bombers on twenty-four-hour airborne alert, 'loitering' near Soviet airspace on the other side of the pole. I'm relieved though puzzled that he isn't cagey about his eavesdropping. And while dismayed as usual by his one-upmanship, I hang on his words, intent on learning more. Jeff listens, nodding and pretending he's heard it all before. But he obviously hasn't and to avoid making a slip that would reveal his ignorance he pokes fun at Danny.

"He probably thinks we mean the pole over there," he snorts, pointing to the totem pole in front of Caribou Hall. Danny says nothing but it's clear that both he and Jeff are complacent about what they've heard.

When they've gone and I'm left cleaning up the mess in my room, the weight of the let-down descends on me. Am I the only one who cares about these things? I've never thought of myself as an oddball but could my fascination with military hardware (which I would have loved to see in action as long as I was not on the receiving end) be morbid? Many years hence, reading the autobiography of a German historian, I'll recognize myself in his recollection of how, as an eleven-year-old boy in 1918, he had run to the wall of the police station every day after school to lap up the authorities' inflated inventory from the front: the miles of territory the Kaiser's troops had conquered, the tons of booty they'd plundered, the hundreds of prisoners they'd taken, etc.

The problem with the Cold War we're in today is that so much of it is hush-hush. Although we know who our enemies are, not all of the massive military build-up is disclosed and people with information worth hearing tend to keep it to themselves. Most others shrug off the entire issue and concentrate on their material well-being instead. It's still a year before Stanley Kubrick will turn Chrome Dome into a public spectacle with the movie *Doctor Strangelove*. Few people have yet come to terms with atomic devices and many aren't comfortable with the idea of having them on Canadian soil. They would be appalled to see the Queen Elizabeth Islands – if they could find them on a map – bristling with radar antennas and strewn with the vapor trails of B-52s carrying nuclear bombs.

Despite the others' cool reception, Dave's demonstration turns out to be a fitting prelude to more revelations in the weeks ahead. The first of these comes the following Friday at school. It's the middle of the afternoon and we're working quietly on cards that each of us has taken from the SRAReading Lab. My difficulties with spelling aside, I'm the third-best reader in the class after Robin and Wendy, who are tied halfway through the orange level. Each card includes a text on a new subject followed by questions, which we answer on a separate sheet. We then present the answers to Miss Sadler, who checks them and notes our scores in an official-looking register. She's usually in a good mood during SRA periods, no doubt because we don't need any disciplining and she can correct math exercises in peace. The card I'm working on is about aliens. I was looking forward to it for some time and am peeved at the author's cowardly conclusion that, if extra-terrestrial beings exist at all, they probably have to have sensors resembling eyes, ears and a nose and, in short, be a lot like us. After ticking off the multiple-choice answers with perfunctory strokes of my pen, I take the sheet up to Miss Sadler and stand waiting for her to finish what she's doing. Her manner is almost congenial. Flipping through the box of correction masks when she's ready, she selects the one for my card and lays it over the answers. I'm relieved to see that only one is wrong—a score enabling me to go on to a new and, hopefully, more investigative article. Miss Sadler tries to circle the mistake with her red pen and, realizing it's out of ink, opens the middle drawer of her desk to take out a new cartridge. My heart freezes: the strap lies flat along the inside edge of the drawer, right in front of me. It's black and scaly like the garter snakes I hate on my grandparents' farm. But a noise at the back of the trailer makes Miss Sadler and me both look up. When she sees who it is her budding congeniality fades. She orders me back to my seat.

The principal, Mr. McAllister, is stamping the snow off his boots. Without removing them, and without saying a word, he strides up the aisle on the girls' side to the front of the room, nodding a curt greeting to Miss Sadler. There is dead silence as he turns to face us, his features rigidly set. He's a tall, broad-shouldered man with greying hair and a pencil moustache. He has a clipped way of speaking, in short bursts. Beth has him as her science teacher and worships him. For us, in the primary grades, he's a bit like the strap: rarely seen and fearsome. His tone is grave.

"Boys and girls," he begins. "I've got some unpleasant news... Something dreadful has happened." We hold our breath, not daring even to twitch. Has there been an accident? A death? Whatever it is must be dire.

"President Kennedy has been shot." He mops his brow with the sleeve of his corduroy suit jacket and waits, either for the announcement to sink in or for inspiration on how to continue.

We're stunned. There is no TV yet in Churchill (a local station will start broadcasting a couple of hours a day next year). But our parents listen to the radio and we've all heard Kennedy's voice on the news. I can visualize his face as well because it caught my eye one day: a handsome, determined face splashed on the front page of the *Winnipeg Free Press*, speaking words quoted boldly in the headline. Why would anyone want to shoot him? Why would anyone want to shoot anyone, unless they've declared war? Is that it? Are we at war? My youthful imagination tears ahead like wildfire.

"Now we don't know what this could lead to..." Mr. McAllister goes on, as if he can read the thoughts racing through my mind. He pauses after each phrase. "But I'm also here to tell the plan... to those of you who are new... And remind those who were here last year... in case it gets serious." My heart is thumping in my chest. Can he hear it? His eyes land on mine for a second. "If the order comes... you'll have to drop whatever you're doing..." he pans our petrified faces, "...get dressed in an orderly manner... but as quickly as possible... Form lines outside... and, when Miss Sadler tells you to, proceed together to the grain elevators... As quickly as possible as a group... Is that clear?"

There's a murmur of assent. I stare at him blankly. Why the grain elevators? Why the plan? Sensing our consternation, but also seeing that the principal is not about to elaborate, Miss Sadler reassures him: "Your instructions are clear, sir. We will all do as we're told."

"I know I can count on you," he concludes. "For now, you are dismissed until Monday... The rest of the day is to mourn President Kennedy... and pray." He bids us good evening and stalks out, leaving a numbing pall of uneasiness behind him.

"You are dismissed," Miss Sadler repeats in the strained silence. "There's no homework this weekend." Normally this pronouncement would rouse a cheer but, in the circumstances, it rings like a limp and lame consolation. We stow our books with slow, deliberate motions as if swimming in a heavy, viscous medium. Still silent, we wait with folded arms on our desks for our names to be called one by one, meaning we can get up and leave.

Outside, I run and catch up to Robin, who's in front of the federal building heading for the RCMP barracks. Panting, I ask him, "What was that about last year?"

Robin hesitates. I can see he knows full well what I'm talking about, so he has likely been mulling it over too. But he's not always forthcoming and, when together with Jeff, can even be a bit surly towards me. He finally volunteers a hurried answer: "He meant the crisis in Cuba… We had a drill… Sorry, I gotta go."

I think for a couple of seconds. And then it hits me. Even in the sleepy, secluded farming village of Norton, I'd felt the tenseness of those days in October 1962. No doubt I overheard Dad and Dave talking. A flash of memory sweeps me back to our grey one-room schoolhouse. I'm sitting with the twins, Terry and Jake, on the window ledge. We aren't supposed to sit there. I'm telling them with stern assurance that there's going to be nuclear war. "Go on," they laugh at me. "That could never happen!" And of course, they were right, as only blithe farm kids can be right. But to me the idea was harrowing and now it anguishes me again.

It's ten o'clock. I should be asleep but I make a point of staying awake until Dave comes to bed. He puts one foot on the edge of my mattress, as he always does, and hauls himself up to his bunk. Sandy, lying by my pillow, is accustomed to this ritual and doesn't move a muscle. He's starting to look mangier and has already lost the tips of his ears to frostbite. By the time we move away, leaving him behind, he'll have nothing but ugly dark nubs on his head like the other cats in Churchill.

"Dave ...?"

"Yeah?"

"If things get bad... Why do they want us to go to the grain elevators?"

"Well..." Like Robin he understands straight away what I mean but now the pause is longer. He's doubtless asking himself how much an eleven-year-old should be told. When his answer finally comes, it surprises me how candid he is. He must have realized I'm growing up. The central block between the silos, he explains, is the only building in town with thick concrete walls. It would be our only hope if the Fort was ever hit by a ballistic missile or a bomb. I shudder, remembering the blinding flash and slowly rising mushroom cloud I saw in a newsreel. But my fear is tantalizing. I have to know more, like the time I spied a sloughed snake skin in the ditch and bent down in loathing curiosity to examine it. I pump Dave for more information, knowing how knowledgeable he is about rocketry.

"What does ballistic mean?" Here he only pauses long enough to gauge how much I've probably understood in his *How and Why Wonder Books*. He gives me a crash course on multi-stage missiles, arched trajectories, re-entry vehicles and thermonuclear warheads. "And why do we have to hurry?" I ask hesitantly, recalling how I studied the black and yellow scales of the snake skin while extending a jittery hand to touch it. There's another pause, this time while Dave considers whether the rest should be censored. The answer, when it comes, is as peremptory as the surprising, paper-like dryness of the reptile's scales under my tensed fingertip: at top speed, Dave reels off from memory, an ICBM can travel four miles a second. Meaning we'd only have half an hour or so from the time it was detected by the DEW line stations. A final fear grips me as I remember how I suddenly recoiled at the thought of the long, scaly band coming alive and jumping up at me.

"What happens if they attack at night?"

"We'd be screwed." He says it as if wiping his hands soberly, as I did while backing away from the sloughed snake skin. "And we'd be screwed anyway, because, for starters, the explosion would be a lot bigger than the one that levelled Hiroshima and, secondly, even if some of us survived, we'd die of radiation sickness if we ventured outside. Now go to sleep!"

I can't for a long time and dwell on this for days. Annihilation is staring us in the face. We're in the front line—no, we're out in the middle of No Man's Land with no cover. In short, we're doomed and the curtain is bound to fall sooner than later. Somewhere in an underground silo in Siberia, an ICBM stands waiting with Fort Churchill's coordinates programmed in its guidance system. The only thing that can save us is if that system is communist junk. And that we can only find out the hard way. Chances are, it's stolen US technology. Robin has told us (quoting his father this time) that there are Russian spies making copies of everything everywhere—even inside the Pentagon.

Oddly, my anxiety finds a vent in resentment against America, an antipathy that comes to a head three Saturdays later. I get up early to go buy Dave's and Beth's Christmas presents in Fort Churchill. The plan is for me to take the nine o'clock bus and come home by lunchtime with Dad, who will be out running errands. He gives me a five-dollar bill, telling me to be careful with it and to meet him in front of the commissary before eleven.

As I trudge down our steps into the wide, vacant street, the packed snow crunches softly under my feet. The sound is a bit muffled this morning and the subarctic gloom isn't brightening. Ice crystals float in the air, lighting on my cheeks like tiny, tingling butterflies. The wind has dashed —the calm before the storm.

The door of the bus stands open but it's empty inside. Moreover, the engine isn't running so the vinyl and metal seats are hard and frigid. I sit on my hands, shivering and worrying that I may have misread the timetable. Just after nine, however, other people start trickling into the bus: bleary-eyed grown-ups on their way to work. They yawn and exchange snatches of stale conversation. The driver sidles up fifteen minutes late and finishes his cigarette unhurriedly by the open door. Judging from the others' indifference, this must be routine behaviour. I'm discovering the indolence of the north, a scourge that I will lose patience with again and again in years to come. When the driver finally climbs in and turns the ignition key, I groan in sympathy with the starter as it whines against the cold, and fret that it will never catch. But it does, after an extended break on the fourth try. The driver rams the gear shift forward and the bus clunks around the piled snow onto the road.

We head out of town onto the tundra and I strain to pick out the few features the barren landscape has to offer. The rocks along the shore are buried in snow. Beyond them, veiled in mist, I can picture the bay spreading frozen and forlorn—a great unmade bed, rumpled where the ice has heaved. Looking around to make sure no one is watching, I pull the fiver out of my pocket and, after unfolding it carefully, pore over each side of it in the twilight. I've never seen a five-dollar bill up close before, nor have I ever held so much money in my hands. Besides the red serial number and black lettering, it's all blue and white. The wintry forest scene on the back casts a peaceful spell over me, an enchantment that isn't broken until we rumble into the base. Again, checking for prying eyes, I fold the banknote into a small square and stuff it deep into my pants pocket, marvelling at the mysterious power projected by money.

Unlike the dingy Bay and cramped S&M store in Churchill, the commissary at the Fort is brightly lit with aisles wide enough for two people to pass abreast. I've been here once before and know exactly where to find the few items that interest me. The five dollars will be evenly split, with two cents left over, as I asked Dave and Beth a week ago what they wanted and they found out my budget from Mom. After inquiring with friends about prices and stock, they gave me clear instructions and a warning not to screw up. Dave, a sports-car enthusiast who already subscribes to *Hot Rod* magazine, wants a scale model of the M&R Top Fuel Dragster or, if it's gone, the Ivo Barnstormer. Beth, a trendy teenybopper who is starting to paint her nails, has her heart set on an LP: either *Annette's Beach Party* by Annette Funicello, or *Blue on Blue* by Bobby Vinton. I find both their first choices within minutes, pausing only to frown quizzically at a curious display in the record rack: a space reserved for what appears to be an eagerly awaited album advertised with a reproduction of its black-and-white cover and a diagonal red band proclaiming *COMING SOON!* Two things puzzle me: the title at the top of the picture, *BEATLEMANIA!* is at odds with the four serious-looking faces underneath; and the distinctly male heads topped with long bangs and hair over their ears. 'What's the world coming to?' Dad will ask himself aloud when this album lands in our house a couple of months from now. I spend the hour I have to spare drooling over the model warships and jet fighters and leafing through the latest Green Lantern comic. He's the only superhero I like because he comes from the sentient planet Mogo, which is neater than Krypton, and there's more integrity in his ring than in any of the preposterous powers of the Justice League pantheon. The problem with Green Lantern comics, though, is that they aren't very tradable. I consider the latest Sad Sack issue, amused by the idea of buying a spoof on the army at a military base. But economics (I will learn one day) is about the choices man makes with limited resources so, with the two pennies change from the presents and the dime I saved from last week's allowance, I pump for the new Archie, knowing I can swap it for three older ones. The pimply-faced young man at the check-out counter, dressed in an Air Force uniform, doesn't even look at the cover. In swift, well-oiled moves he rings up my purchases, slips my fiver and dime into the till, slams it shut, tears off the receipt and hands it to me without a word.

It's a quarter to eleven when I come out of the commissary. Dad is waiting for me down the street in his blue Ford with the doors marked *Indian & Northern Affairs* in orange lettering. Rolling down the window, he urges me with a wave to hurry. He wants to beat the blizzard and still has to stop in Camp 10, he tells me as I climb in. The wind has indeed picked up and is starting to gust in sudden fits. The sky is moreover dusky for this time of day as we set out on the road back to town. I'm silent, having suddenly remembered a dream from the night before in which Dad kept telling me I was getting nice notes from girls. God, he can even gross me out in my dreams! Actually, we have few opportunities to be alone together and don't know each other all that well. No doubt he still thinks of me as a child who likes building Tinker Toy towns, not as a thinker on the cusp of adolescence.

By now the rocks along the bay are barely visible. The eleven o'clock news is ending on the radio. As a mental exercise I try to follow the last item, about the conclusion of a long-running court case in Japan. The judges finally ruled that the Tokyo government owes no compensation to the victims of the atomic bombings of Hiroshima and Nagasaki because the United States violated international law by inflicting unnecessary pain on cities of no military significance. The flattened desolation of Hiroshima flashes through my mind. Surely the court is right: the heartless Americans should never have dropped atomic bombs on civilians. But then I have another thought: since the people of Hiroshima and Nagasaki were innocent victims, shouldn't the court have awarded them compensation anyway? The announcer has the last word, noting in a parting shot at the Japs that today is the twenty-second anniversary of the sneak attack on Pearl Harbour. There is no doubt as to whose side he's on. I can feel my resentment rising.

We drive along the airport perimeter and my heart skips a beat. Only a couple of hundred yards from us, inside the chain-link fence with a large white sign marked *Department of National Defence KEEP OUT,* a small jet is manoeuvring to enter the hangar. When it swings its tail around and stops to wait for the doors to be opened, I can just make out the star-and-bars roundel of the US Air Force on the fuselage. I tense up and scowl. Dad has his eyes on the road but must have seen the plane out of the corner of his eye.

"Looks like he's holing up till the storm blows over."

I don't answer. We pass Camp 20, the Inuit village, a tidy cluster of log-cabin-style houses. They look quite recent from what I can see of them. Dad tells me the settlement is also called Akudlik, a name that would normally appeal to me, like Inuktitut, which I often roll around my tongue, savouring the 'k' and the 't's, 'i's and 'u's. But not now.

"Anything wrong?" Dad asks.

"What are they doing here?"

"What are who doing here?" He shoots back, slowing sharply as a sheet of blowing snow slams into my side of the car.

"The plane back at the airport. It was American."

"They're our allies," he answers distractedly, as if this might be news to me. Which makes me more indignant still.

"This is our country," I lash out. "Why should we get killed because of them? And why should we mourn their president? Why don't they go home and leave us alone?"

Now it's Dad's turn to be silent for a moment. "Watch the side of the road, will you?" he cautions as we drive by HMCS Churchill, which is not a ship but a low building with a water tower behind it. Unknown to me, its purpose is to intercept radio signals from remote points further north and relay them to receiving stations in Ottawa and elsewhere. Some of the operators are there to listen in on the Russians.

"Yankee go home," Dad muses after thinking a moment. I search his face, wondering if he could be taunting me, but actually he's reminiscing. "That's how a lot of Brits felt during the war." Dad spent three years in Yorkshire with an RCAF bomber squadron, humbly, as a ground mechanic. He ate slop and lost some of his teeth. "Overpaid, oversexed and over here, they used to say too," he chuckles. I wince at the word 'oversexed'. He rarely talks about the war. I know he went over in 1942 on the *Queen Elizabeth II*, painted grey and refitted as a troop transport. "Like walking into the side of a mountain," he has told us a couple of times. "No convoy could keep up with her so she travelled alone, zigzagging to dodge U-boats." This impresses me because I know it must have been scary. But otherwise, his war years sound painfully dull compared with the pitched battles that Jeff's dad fought in, or even the military police service of Robin's father in France after D-Day. "I'll tell you a story about the Americans," Dad offers. My ears prick up. Is he going to tell a real yarn for once? Is he going to dramatize about how the US military's numbers turned the tide of the war and gave everyone new hope of getting home alive? "One day they got this sudden craving for ice cream."

"Ice cream…" I can feel my anticipation deflating like a punctured tire. "I scream, you scream…" the corny rhyme echoes hollowly in my head.

"The weather was hot for once and the whole US squadron next door wanted ice cream. Keep an eye on the ditch." We've slowed to a crawl, but even at this speed he grips the wheel with both hands to counter the driving snow. "So, they pooled their pay and made the rounds of the local farms," he continues. "I don't know how they managed it, with food so tight, but they came back with five big pails of cream. Another detail scoured the woods for wild strawberries. Then they collected chocolate rations and commandeered the whole supply of sugar and vanilla in the mess tent. An Italian guy among them whipped that all up into a dozen gallons of ice cream in three flavours. They took it up to thirty thousand feet in a Flying Fortress and circled till the stuff was frozen solid." I wait for some kind of punch line but none comes.

"Is that it?" I ask finally. He can sense my disappointment.

"Yes, that's the story, such as it is. It says something about them." But nothing about the war, I think dismally.

The car shudders as the wind scores another broadside hit. A mile before reaching town we turn off the road into Camp 10, the

Chipewyan settlement. As I will learn years from now, both these terms are borrowed: Chipewyan is a Cree word describing the band's traditional dress while Camp 10 is a carry-over from the army's 1940s designation of this site. It has no prettier name.

The township consists of several rows of plywood houses half the size of ours. They could have been white originally but the weather-beaten paint is now grey and peeling. They'd be better called shacks. Some have a boarded-up window or a ragged tent pitched behind the back porch. The camp looks deserted and ghostly between the sheets of blowing snow. Dad stops the car and gets out next to a shack with a derelict sled sticking out of the snowbank in front. A tiny lean-to clinging to the side is so low I think it has to be a doghouse, until a hand pushes back the square of animal hide nailed to the opening. An old woman dressed in a torn duffle jacket creeps halfway out on all fours, her wizened face bundled in a soiled yellow headscarf. As she and Dad exchange greetings, a man who must have heard them unsteadily thrusts open the door of the shack and supports himself against it with his shoulder while clutching a liquor bottle in his other hand. I feel uncomfortable. Long, unkempt hair curls over the collar of his red and black checked shirt, a corner of which hangs listlessly over his frayed jeans. He stands half a foot taller than Dad but his massive frame is belied by a look of defeat in his unsmiling eyes, which gaze over Dad's head into empty space. At first, he seems to be trying to get his bearings in a thick fog while Dad delivers what begins as a harangue and ends with an entreaty. At this point the man seems to wake from his apathy and loses patience. Taking a swig from his bottle, he starts interrupting. His expression grows hostile. Soon they're arguing and shaking their heads adamantly in turn. A boy aged six or seven appears in the doorway. He's sucking at something shapeless, a piece of gristle maybe, unfazed by the men's heated words. Apparently, he's used to shouting. We stare at each other through the windshield. I can't decide whether he's the same boy I saw at the garbage dump in September, poking through the sour-smelling heaps of smouldering ashes and blackened tin cans. I press my presents to my chest and look away. When Dad gets back into the car, he stamps the snow off his feet angrily. Swearing under his breath, using the 'f' word (it's not like him), he yanks the gearshift into reverse and backs bumpily up the narrow street to the road.

We don't speak the rest of the way into town, each of us harried by our own demons. After stopping to help a driver with a wheel in the ditch, and more cursing, we finally reach home well after twelve o'clock. By this time the storm is a chained beast, stomping, snorting and straining to tear loose on a rampage. I struggle to keep my balance, walking backwards from the car so as not to face the pelting, stinging blasts of wind. Inside the porch, Dad composes himself as he pulls off his duffle-lined Eskimo parka with bands of embroidery round the waist and sleeves. "This is gonna be one hell of a blow," he announces to Mom and Beth in the living room. The house groans and shudders as if in assent. Mom takes my purchases and spirits them away to a hiding place, not so much for the pretence of surprise as to ensure they won't be tampered with before Christmas. I give Beth the thumbs-up sign.

The blizzard is a whiteout that lasts three days. We're told on the radio to stay indoors. Neither Jeff's house nor the federal building, each about twenty feet away, is visible through our windows. The wind is incessant, roaring in from the bay with awesome power. At times it threatens to reach under the floor, lift us off the beams that hold us above the permafrost and blow us away, like Dorothy and her dog in *The Wizard of Oz*. How I would love to be swept away and deposited in a land with no Bomb, no strap and no bath night! My new Archie comic has wrinkles by the end of the afternoon but I only come out of my room when Dave wins the fight for the record player and puts on *Johnny Horton's Greatest Hits*. He can play Sink the Bismarck, The Battle of New Orleans and North to Alaska as long and often as he wants. I revel in their heroic choruses. But I draw a line between melodrama and mush, so the second time Comanche comes around I go back to my room to build a Meccano crane.

The next day is painfully long. Normally after breakfast Mom would drag Dave, Beth and me to mass at the Anglican Church (Dad is a lapsed Catholic and gets to stay at home). Instead, while she knits and putters around with Beth in the kitchen, Dad, Dave and I listen to Sunday Morning Magazine on the radio, hearing Lyndon Johnson's Texan drawl for the first time. Dad is intrigued by a story from Iraq, a country I've never heard of, where the government is requiring Jews to register within ninety days or lose their citizenship and have their property confiscated. The Holocaust has been overshadowed by the Cold War and won't be the focus of public attention for another generation, but Dad tells us we had Jewish ancestors in Poland. I go to find Iraq on Dave's globe. When I come back, the topic on the radio is the 'replay' of a touchdown in a big football game on American TV yesterday. We're told that the announcer unwittingly created a sensation and a new feature by asking a technician to rewind the video tape so viewers could thrill to the spectacle a second time (he warned them that what they were about to see was Not a new touchdown). A lot is happening with mass media these days, so much that we can't see the forest for the trees. Marshall McLuhan is writing about it but I won't read

The Gutenberg Galaxy for several years. And when I do, I'll confuse his tribal base with the sixties generation's burgeoning band of songwriters and political activists. Many more years from now, I'll wonder if the move from individualism to the global village (which McLuhan sees driven by the "electronic interdependence of media") hasn't been turned on its head by Facebook and Twitter.

Beth gets a game of Monopoly going in the afternoon but I soon lose all my money and hole up in my room again, this time to build a Tinker Toy drum set. I mull over what I've seen and heard in the past weeks. When there's nothing more to do but go to bed early, I pull the covers over my head, willing sleep to come and shut out the perplexity that has worked me into a state of agitation. Perhaps I squeeze Sandy unconsciously or annoy him with my tossing and turning: when I awake around midnight he's gone. The wind howls. The house shakes. I get up, go to the window and run a finger along the crack between the sill and the bottom of the frame, pondering the dream that woke me up. An icy cold creep in where the weather stripping has worn thin. It's pitch black in the room. The dream was a nightmare about Dad and me. At first, I thought we were back in the car, buffeted by the rising storm. But the windshield and dashboard were bigger, and all of a sudden, I realized we were in an airplane fighting turbulence. 'Watch the starboard wingtip!' Dad told me, his eyes surveying the instruments and the darkening sky ahead. His brow was furrowed, his jaw thrust forward. He had to shout because of the din of the engines. Looking to my right I gulped: we were in a bomber, flying in formation! I glanced at the altimeter at the centre of the display and gulped again; the oversized, oneiric numbers told me we were at thirty thousand feet!

"Where are we headed?" I yelled, terrified.

"Camp 10!"

"Camp 10? You wanna bomb Camp 10?" There was no answer. He was struggling to keep the plane level while listening to a message in his headset. My terror turned to horror as I pictured the lines of peeling shacks torched by incendiaries. "You can't do that!" I screamed. "Moses and Janie are down there! What did they ever do to us?" Dad remained stone-faced. It was true what people say: he looks a bit like John Wayne.

"We're not going to bomb them, just drop leaflets," he assured me finally, his eyes now shifting from the gyro horizon to the airspeed indicator.

"Leaflets?"

"Yes, leaflets! Telling them to surrender. Those are my orders."

"But why do they have to surrender? We're not at war."

"You don't know the half of it," was all he would say. Ahead of us, eerie blue beams crisscrossed the sky – searchlights! – and I thought I saw a flash of anti-aircraft fire. The nightmare ended there. Did I scream out loud? Apparently not, judging from Dave's steady breathing from the upper bunk.

The chill from the window reminds me where I am and that no one could survive beyond these two fragile panes of glass. It can get colder here than on parts of Mars, as the probes will tell us when they start landing there. I crawl reluctantly back into bed, fretting that the oil stove will fail and leave us all to freeze slowly in our sleep.

Is that why I'm shaking?

Childhood fears are notoriously overblown, but when we're in their grip there's no telling what is real. Dad's right: I don't know the half of it. I'm just a kid and we've only lived in this town for a few months. I'll learn more about what's going on in later years, some of it even decades from now on the internet. In the untiring flow of history, Churchill's destiny is and will always be shaped by far-away mainstream forces over which it has no control. Its blinking moment in the Cold War limelight will be brief. Now, in the early sixties, there's no doubt the Soviets still have us in their crosshairs. The Fort is the largest joint Canadian-US military facility ever built, and as the most direct forward refuelling station with an airstrip long enough to land a B-52, it's worth knocking out by some means. But unknown to most people the situation is changing. The Pearson government is bent on merging, downsizing and closing bases. And while the Liberals are more cooperative with the US than the Conservatives were about overflights and a nuclear deterrent, submarines and land-based missiles are replacing long-range bombers and satellites are taking over from reconnaissance planes. As a consequence, Churchill is losing its geographic advantage. HMCS Churchill, which in the mid1950s accommodated up to twenty radio operators including the first WRENs to serve in the north, will be decommissioned in 1968. The rocket research range to the south will be turned into a Northern Studies centre in 1976. Fort Churchill will be shut down and bulldozed in 1980, its amenities replaced by the town of Churchill's humongous Centre Complex. So ultimately, today's doomsayers will be right though for the wrong reason: the Fort will indeed be reduced to rubble but by obsolescence, not by a Russian ICBM. The dread of nuclear annihilation that dances like a demon in my head will be subdued by long familiarity and eventually laid to rest. Yet it will continue to twitch in its grave when poked. Like the day, many years hence, when I'll take shelter from a downpour in a park while cycling in ex-East Germany. Removing my helmet to wipe my eyes I'll gasp and shrink from the sight, not ten feet away, of the red sickle and hammer embossed on a Soviet war memorial. For a split-second I'll be convulsed by the thought of the buried soldiers springing out to pack me off to a labour camp in Siberia! As long as I live, the old iron symbols of the Cold War will never lose their power to cow me.

Camp 10 will likewise be abandoned but with no anti-climax. It's already a full-blown tragedy the scale of which I won't really measure before reading about it in a sociology course at college. Until then I will suppose (who knows why?) that the Chipewyan were relocated here because their land was being flooded for a dam project, a recurring story in the current period of hydroelectric development. The actual reason was a decision, prompted by paternalism and a miscalculation that will be described as one of the most grievous errors ever committed by the federal government. The Chipewyan were moved to Churchill in 1956 from their settlement at Little Duck Lake, over two hundred miles to the northwest, because the trading post they relied on there had become unprofitable and the Hudson's Bay Company was anxious to close it. At the same time, the wildlife authorities believed that the caribou population, the mainstay of the Indians' diet, was dwindling whereas the herd was healthy. So they've been here ever since, dumped in an area where they have no ancestral attachment and no livelihood, housed in a flimsily built township bordering the graveyard. Driven to drink by idleness, they trade their macaroni rations for booze, neglect their children and fight over women and living space. Unknown to me, it is a maelstrom of starvation, house fires, murder and rape that Dad has been given charge of. I'll wonder in future years if he had any idea what he was getting into.

The blizzard rages on another full day but it could be any number of days. I've lost track of time. Dave tells me it's Tuesday morning. We can hear that the wind has abated and the sky appears to be brightening, though we still can't see anything through the snow and ice crusted on the storm windows. Nor can we open the doors. The back one is no surprise, having already been half-blocked before the blizzard by the snowdrift behind the house. But now, the front one won't budge either. Armed with shovels, Dad and Dave crawl through the living-room window and drop waist-deep into the snow that has piled up between our house and the federal building. The work is exhausting but after going at it in turns for a couple of hours, they dig a trench around the corner of the house to the front porch. When they finally yank the door open, I pull on my boots and parka and step out into a world transformed. There are no more discernible streets, just the upper halves of buildings poking up here and there like flotsam on a sea of white. The town is buried in three feet of snow. The only other figure to be seen is Jeff's father, who hasn't yet freed their front door. When he returns Dad's call of encouragement with a desultory wave, I can see he's wearing his signature striped sweater under his open parka. Every half hour I relieve Dad with the shovelling, widening the gallery that Dave is cutting towards our former street. We can hear the snowplough working near the railway line but by nightfall it hasn't even started down the street in front of The Bay. It won't clear La Verendrye Street until late tomorrow, leaving eight-foot walls of snow on either side with just enough space between them for two vehicles to pass. We spend Thursday digging out a driveway for the car, which refuses to start.

    School doesn't resume until the following Monday. As we line up to enter our trailer, I wonder what's happened to Danny, who hasn't shown up. I'm relieved to be in class again though, a feeling I can read in the others' faces as well: we're back in a setting where time is filled for us rather than consuming us with its longing for repletion. Miss Sadler actually seems glad to see us, proof that boredom can make the heart grow fonder. She says she's going to bring Christmas ornaments this week and asks if a couple of us can help her deck the walls of our trailer after class on Friday. Sandra and Astrid, both avid joiners, put up their hands before Wendy can beat them to it. They offer to add leftover baubles and tinsel to Miss Sadler's garlands and Santa cut-outs. Come Friday afternoon, Jeff and Roger are intent on spoiling their visible excitement. While Miss Sadler is busy at the back out of earshot, they taunt Sandra by speculating, just loud enough for the rest of us to hear, on what will happen if a tubby person climbs on their desks to hang decorations. The putative damage escalates with each dig and causes me to crack up noisily. Miss Sadler silences me with a cross "Ben, stop that!" so I'm not surprised when, after God Save the Queen, Jeff and Roger are dismissed before me. Only Sandra, Astrid and I are left in the room with Miss Sadler, who says nothing to me (letting me meditate on my bad behaviour, I presume). She tells the girls to measure the garlands and count the ornaments and Santas. At last, when I'm starting to get fidgety, she turns to me and explains: I'm to wait while she makes a list of homework to take to Danny, who hasn't been at school since the blizzard.

"Is he sick?" I ask.

"I saw his mother at lunchtime. She told me he might not come back for a while."

This worries me. With nothing else to do, I watch Sandra and Astrid take stock of the decorations and the available space. This is the first time I've been privy to a conversation between two girls and it strikes me that, though lacking a normal sense of humour, they are more cooperative than boys; as if they had less to prove or compete for. I also find it amazing how they can keep up such a constant, easy banter. Astrid is talking about a scarf she's knitting for her sister, with 'oohs' and 'ahs' from Sandra who hasn't learned to make jacquard patterns yet. What a far cry from the roughhousing and jibes that Jeff, Robin, Danny and I can indulge in! Miss Sadler at last calls me to her desk and hands me the list, telling me to collect the books Danny will need from his desk. As I pull them out of the drawer under his seat a new concern crosses my mind: will I be able to find his house? I've only been there once, to watch him mend his fishing net on the back porch. Even in normal times the shacks in the Flats all look the same. Now it's dark and they're covered in snow, some to the rooftop. As I head up the street, scarcely wide enough for a single car, I see that in a couple of cases the occupants have given up on clearing their doorway and are using the gable window to climb in and out. Getting my bearings from the faint outline of the whale plant two hundred yards further on, I trudge up the steps of the shack in the likeliest position and knock. When no one answers, I lift the latch and enter the porch. "Danny!" I yell, knocking again on the inner door. There's a movement behind it.

"Who is it?" a woman's voice calls. Danny's mother, I gamble.

"It's Ben. I've got homework for Danny. From school…" I add pointlessly. The knob turns and the door opens. She observes me with dark eyes almost level with mine. This close, the set lips can't overshadow their softness. I feel shy and uncomfortable.

"Danny!" she shouts, adding something in French. I survey the living-room furnishings: a sofa, an armchair, a record player with an Inuit carving on top and a beaded Indian wall hanging that looks like a turtle. A tangy smell of wild meat hangs in the air.

She has to call a second time before one of the two doors to the left opens and Danny emerges from the dim interior. He approaches wordlessly, his eyes downcast. They look swollen.

"What's the matter?" I ask as his mother slips away to the kitchen, leaving us together on the threshold. "Are you sick or what?" He avoids my gaze. "Miss Sadler made a list of homework for you," I explain, unzipping my binder and handing him his books one by one. He still says nothing. "I had trouble finding…"

"It's Nicky," Danny interrupts me finally. I sense the gravity in his voice.

"What about Nicky?" As if to ward off what might be coming, I conjure up a recollection of the day Danny took him home from Jeremy's kennel, the gangly pup straining on the rope leash, unable to walk a straight line. And the day I played fetch with him, here on the back porch, while Danny mended his net. The little pup kept misjudging the distance, running too far, slamming on the brakes, wheeling round and looking frantically for the stick that was caught between his hind legs. How we laughed at his antics!

"They shot him."

"What?"

"The Mounties!" Danny blurts between sobs. "The day before the storm."

"The Mounties shot him…" I repeat his words in disbelief. "Why would they do that?" I can't help thinking of President Kennedy. Danny isn't listening.

"They lied. They said they thought he was a stray but they knew he was my dog." His face is stricken. "I found the spot. I saw the blood…"

Robin

Churchill, January 1964

We rang in the New Year at a Hawaiian party put on by the RCMP in Caribou Hall. Featured were paper flower garlands, loud shirts, wavering strains of slide guitar blaring from a jukebox and bowls of pineapple punch labelled *Non-alcoholic* and *Alcoholic*. Despite the best efforts of Robin's mom to limit consumption of the latter, the party grew rowdier as the night wore on. At one point the most boisterous group, led by a tall guy with a crew-cut and twin mickeys in the pockets of his baggy Bermuda shorts, grabbed a young Mountie whose naked, muscular arms and torso were smeared with Coppertone, and tried to drag him outside to throw him into the snow. To no avail.

"He knows karate," Robin observed admiringly as the Mountie flung his assailants aside one by one. If Robin's comment was meant for me, then it was the first time he'd spoken to me directly for half an hour. Nor did he show much interest in the few things I pointed out to him, intent instead on keeping up a running dialogue with the younger adults who indulged him and on getting the attention of my sister Beth and her friend Sheila, who were both after bigger game. Robin knew that I knew why he was giving me the cold shoulder, but the issue had become taboo and this was no place to hash it out again. So, we stood in the corner, in limbo between the older kids who were dancing and the younger ones who had been left at home with a babysitter—an estranged couple transformed into wallflowers, each putting up a pretence of having fun.

That was Monday night. Since then, we've spent the afternoons playing hockey on the outdoor rink. Jeff might have come to my place to play war but not Robin, and without Danny it wouldn't have been the same. Here at the rink Robin is practically ignoring me altogether while bantering with Jeff, Roger and the older boys including Lennie, who blames Danny for what happened at the theatre and in the meantime has dumped Wendy, all of which sits very favourably with Jeff. The hockey games don't offer much consolation, since the older boys hog the puck and I'm not the scrappy type who races into the corners to dig it out. I'm ashamed of the new stick I got for Christmas, which hardly has a nick on it. If only Danny were here, he would feed me the occasional pass and help even the balance with the others. It occurs to me that he's the only real friend I've made since coming to this town four months ago.

School starts up again the following Monday. As we mill in front of the trailer waiting for Miss Spencer to ring the bell, I watch for Danny's slim, sturdy figure ambling down the road. Surely, he has gotten over the loss of Nicky by now. But he doesn't show up and doesn't come to school all week, so, on Friday I volunteer to take more homework to him. If I haven't paid him another visit since before Christmas, it's because to me the Flats are still a psychological remove from the town proper and I need an added pretext to go there.

Danny opens the living-room door after my second knock. He's alone and although he doesn't invite me in, his manner is less despondent than last time. His face even brightens when I ask what he's been up to. He has just come back from a week in the bush, he tells me, pointing proudly to a pair of snowshoes and duffle-lined moccasins in the corner of the porch. He was at the winter camp he has told me about, the one set up by his mother's friend, five miles upriver. They fished through the ice of the lake and hunted rabbits and ptarmigan, which they ate with bannock, beans and warm tea. They also set traps and caught a marten.

"Are you still mad about Nicky?"

"Of course, I am." There's a reproachful edge in his voice, as if I've forgotten he has feelings. For a time, he talks vehemently about the killing while I say little, letting him vent his anger. Then his gaze turns wistful. "Someday I'll have a camp of my own with a sled and a team of purebred dogs. With what Andrew is teaching me I know I can survive on my own." The assertion makes me envious for he indeed sounds capable. What's more, he and this Andrew fellow seem to have developed a close rapport during their time together. Danny may not have a real dad but he has found a valuable surrogate.

"Are you going back there?"

"Not if Mom can help it. She let me go to take my mind off Nicky for a while. But she says I can't miss any more school."

"So, we'll see you on Monday, then."

"Looks that way."

"It'll be nice to have you back… For most of us anyway," I add while turning to leave. It's true: apart from a small faction led by Robin, the class sympathizes with him for the loss of his dog. Danny is actually quite popular as he can be very entertaining when he opens up and is a more congenial clown than either Jeff or Roger. His mimicry and body language have had everyone in stitches, like the time he put on a brief Elvis the Pelvis performance while standing in front. Even Wendy – who normally disapproves of his antics, as much out of loyalty to Miss

Sadler as her own priggishness – cracked up like the rest of us, only to stifle her laughter when she realized that Sad Face was glaring at her.

It turns out, however, that I'm the one who will be absent from school come Monday. My head is starting to ache as I trudge back through the Flats. The shacks are still half-hidden behind the ramparts of snow, though all have shovelled walkways now except for a couple that look deserted. A sweet smell of wood smoke takes the bite off the air. Here on the edge of town the stars sparkle like diamonds sprayed on a black velvet curtain. I'm hoping to see a glimmer of northern lights despite the early hour but there are none as yet. When I reach home, my throat is parched and even after drinking several glasses of water and milk the dryness remains. The next morning, I feel dizzy and feverish. Mom tells me to stay in bed. By Sunday morning a rash has broken out on my chest.

"Did you eat anything unusual?" Mom asks.

"Not that I can remember."

"I hope it's not typhoid," says Beth. There was a small outbreak of the disease recently and we were told to boil our drinking water as a precaution. "Maybe it's that fleabag of a cat you sleep with. He's starting to wander all over town. Someone saw him down by the station last week."

"He hasn't got fleas!" I protest. If cats could be canonized, I would have written letters to the Pope ages ago.

"Then it would be typhus, not typhoid," Dave weighs in. "We learned that in biology. And you're right, that cat is looking lousier by the day." I throw a punch at his stomach that he easily deflects. "You stay away!" he warns and I can tell he's serious.

"I'm going to call the doctor tomorrow," Mom says. "In any case you're staying home. And until further notice, Sandy doesn't come past the front porch."

"But he'll freeze!" I implore her.

"He spends most of the day outside anyway. Apparently, he can fend for himself." It appals me how, all of a sudden, our beloved pet can be shunned as an unsavoury character but clearly there will be no discussion. The judgment passed on me is almost as severe: I'm to be quarantined until the typhus hypothesis is disproved. Dave takes his mattress to the living room but sounds remorseful about the typhus scare.

"I'll bring you a couple of books from the library," he offers.

The next morning the rash has spread to my forehead. Mom looks worried after taking my temperature. She tells me not to scratch so I press the bedsheet to my bumps and grit my teeth. To pass the time, I memorize the names of the thirty-odd hockey players whose pictures Dave has plastered on the walls of our bedroom. Normally I would never doze off during the daytime, despite my predilection for reverie, but the fever causes me to fall into a fitful sleep just below the threshold of consciousness. I'm aware of this because, even as I begin to dream, it's as if I knew that all I have to do is open my eyes to surface. We're playing hockey on the outdoor rink. I don't recall ever seeing the other participants before but on the face of it that is no issue. The weather is bright and sunny for once, so bright it hurts the eyes to look at the surrounding snowbanks. A gaggle of girls are skating around the outer edge of the ice, clinging to each other's scarves. One of them screams when a slapshot grazes her skate. The shooter's face lights up with a fiendish grin. There's something odd about his features and, taking a harder look, I realize that he and the others aren't real boys: they resemble mechanized puppets. Moreover, rather than hockey the game we're playing is an elaborate pattern of weaving and passing, like clockwork. I watch, intent on fitting into this pattern, and two things become clear as I'm drawn into it. The first is that even while circling back and sideways, we're advancing inexorably towards the goal at the far end of the rink, marked by two blocks of snow. The second thing I note is that the aim of the game consists in intricately setting up the ever-changing centre, who shoots when the puck finally reaches him. But as I cross into the other end and approach this lead position, the unobstructed view makes my jaw drop. The goalie, beneath his parka, is a short, furry creature with a long snout which he keeps wiping with his left paw. At last, I can make out why: his snout is bleeding profusely. The ice in front of him is covered with red blotches. Then I see that half his left leg is missing and he's propping himself up with his goalie's stick! A wicked wrist shot slams into his left shoulder, nearly knocking him off balance and raising a wave of hurrahs from my ghoulish companions. My muscles tighten with the realization that my turn to shoot is coming up next. The puck is crossing the ice. It's on my stick and it's no ordinary puck: it bristles with razor-sharp blades! The furry little goalie has his beady black eyes trained on me and I can see they're glistening with terror. I won't do it! I throw down my stick and flee the dream by kicking and flailing my way to the surface. I awake to the benevolent movie-star maw of Boom-Boom Geoffrion smiling down from the wall.

Around three o'clock Mom ushers in the doctor, a middle-aged man with wavy hair. He examines me through dark-rimmed glasses, breathing noisily behind a facemask, and asks if I've experienced any abdominal pain or backache. I haven't.

"Is it typhoid or typhus?" Mom is keen to ascertain.

"No, definitely not," he reassures her. "And it doesn't look like an allergy either. I'd say chickenpox."

"But there's no chickenpox going around."

"There have been a few cases at the base. Were you there over Christmas?"

"Yes, we all went to the party at the officers' mess on Boxing Day." Dad, as a federal civil servant and war veteran, gets invited to most official functions. I remember the long buffet table laden with lukewarm turkey, stuffing, gravy, mashed potatoes, assorted pies and jiggly mint jelly.

"Well, there you go," the doctor concludes. "The incubation period was longer than usual but I'm pretty sure of my diagnosis." I don't tell them how I roughhoused with some air force boys in the cloakroom. One of them tied his scarf over my face. "Have your other kids had it?"

Mom thinks a second. "Yes, when Beth was a baby. So, Ben missed it." This irks me. I missed a lot of things by being born so late.

The doctor is already packing his bag. "You'll need Calamine lotion. And he'll have to stay home from school for ten days. I won't be coming back unless some complication develops."

When they've gone, I lie back and heave a deep sigh of dismay. Good grief! I was already cooped up during the blizzard and desperate to go back to school during those miserable hockey games. Now this! I want to stuff that air force fart's scarf down his pox-ridden throat!

Thankfully, Dave keeps his word and brings me two hardcover books after school: *Assignment in Space* and *Ripcord!* "You'll see, they're right up your alley," he enthuses, laying them on the bed beside me. The glossy cover illustrations lift my battered spirits straight away. The first shows a stricken spaceship hurtling to the surface of an alien world while the second portrays skydivers performing acrobatics in freefall. I'm duly thrilled and tell Dave so.

But I'm not off the hook regarding schoolwork. Mom has lost no time informing Miss Sadler of my illness and the next morning inquires with Robin's mother whether he has ever had chickenpox. He has, so on Wednesday at four o'clock he calls with homework. Mom, who has no inkling of the rift between us, escorts him cheerfully to the doorway of my room. I can see the folded slips of paper protruding from my English, math, geography and science books under his arm. Those will be Miss Sadler's instructions in her even, slanted hand. Robin eyes me warily. He nods a greeting, takes two steps inside to lay the books at the foot of my bed and backs away. Still giving me the silent treatment, I conclude. Until it occurs to me that he might be flustered by my sunken cheeks and Calamine-painted blisters.

"I must be a sorry sight."

"I've seen better."

Before he can say he's in a hurry to leave, I take the initiative.

"Sit down a minute," I plead with him. "I haven't talked to anybody except the cat for three days." Sandy is allowed back in my room but always wants out, the ungrateful wretch.

Robin hesitates. Is he mollified by my supplication? "Well, I guess I can stay for a bit..." he mumbles, still standing in the doorway.

"Dave gave me a couple of really neat books to read." I hold up *Assignment in Space*, brandishing the front cover. "This one is about a crew of astronauts who go to retrieve an asteroid made of pure thorium. They have to bring it to Earth so it can be cut up and used in nuclear reactors."

"Where's the asteroid?"

"In the asteroid belt." I can see he's thinking. "Between Mars and Jupiter."

"I know where it is. I was just wondering how plausible the story might be." That's Robin for you: always ready to poke holes in other people's theories. He wants to be a criminal investigator when he grows up. In a big city like Toronto. "Pure thorium…" He pushes back his curly light brown hair, conscious as ever of his good looks. "That's pretty far-fetched but if they say so, for the sake of the plot…" His scepticism irritates me, though in fact it's a part of him I grudgingly admire. He knows a lot. Unlike Danny or Jeff, he doesn't need an explanation about orbital mechanics or fissionable material.

"But they have to fight the Connies to take possession of the asteroid." I leaf back through the pages in search of the one illustrating the rocket launcher that the crew have set up in a clearing surrounded by rocky crags.

"Connies?"

"Yeah, the Consolidation of Planetary Governments," I babble on in excitement. "They're the enemy. Rip Foster's crew are on the good side, with the Federation of Free Governments…" Robin's snicker trips me up in mid-stride. "What's so funny?"

"Don't you see? Connies is a thin disguise for Commies. Of course, they're the enemy."

"Commies… You mean communists?" I can sense my enthusiasm wobbling and starting to sputter, like when Dad told me his ice-cream story. Only this time I feel foolish because it's obvious. Robin is right, why didn't I see through it? The Connies' angular helmets and arrow-shaped spaceship suddenly look more contrived than sinister.

"Now you've gone and spoiled the book for me."

"Well, I can't help it if you're easily led. Or wishy-washy."

"Who are you calling wishy-washy?"

"That's what my mom says."

"Huh?" I conjure up a vision of his mother's permanent scowl. It's just like her to put me down in her stuck-up British accent. She has never forgiven me for refusing to attend Sunday school. She thinks Mom is too permissive with us. But why should she bother about me? "…You mean about Nicky…" Here we go again—back onto the subject that drove a wedge between us before Christmas.

"I mean about you taking Danny's side against the police."

I groan. We already went through this twice and I know the Mounties' side of the story by heart. Half a dozen dogs were running loose and they were getting meaner and hungrier. One day they harassed a couple of kids on their way to school, nipping at their legs until an older boy drove them off by throwing chunks of ice at them. With a blizzard coming, Robin's dad reckoned, those dogs would be starving and desperate. He sent the two junior Mounties out with rifles to shoot them and burn the carcasses at the dump. They found the pack with Nicky among them on the outskirts of town, fighting over a dead animal. They got them all but one.

"Nicky was neither a stray nor dangerous," I insist for the third time, repeating Danny's argument. "And he was a purebred Eskimo Dog, not an ugly mongrel. That should've been evident."

"Well, he should've been tied up like the dogs in town," Robin snaps back—a well-aimed slur against the Flats.

What really infuriates him is the charge that the police have been shooting dogs ruthlessly since the early days of Camp 10, when canines were allegedly slaughtered as a way to keep the Chipewyan settled by eliminating their means of transport. This claim was brought up at school by Janie, who told us her parents sorely missed the team they'd used in winter to reach a fishing camp on the north side of the river.

Yet Robin won't buy any of this and is sore with me for believing it. What's more, he can sense my deeper grievance, namely that having fondled and played with Nicky as a pup I can't bring myself to think of the killing as anything short of monstrous. I try a new angle that Danny unveiled to me the previous Friday.

"That young Mountie, the one who knows karate... What's his name?"

"Bart."

"Danny heard he's trigger-happy. He came up north just so he could use his gun..."

"That's a lie!" Robin cuts me off angrily. "Danny doesn't know Bart at all! And you don't know what he and Iver have to put up with, the fights at the beer parlour and out in Camp 10."

"They have to break up fights in Camp 10?"

"All the time, and really vicious ones. They never go out there without brass knuckles anymore." I wince. The scene I witnessed in December reassembles in my mind and I want to describe it to Robin, if only to counter that he's not the only one who sees things from the inside. But he pre-empts me yet again. "You wanna hear something about your mild-mannered friend Moses?"

"He's not my friend."

"Well, you stick up for him too. For your information his dad is one of the biggest drunks in the camp. He was ready to kill his brother once over a bottle he'd smashed. Lucky Bart and Iver were nearby to answer another call. Otherwise, there would've been a murder that night. They're not trigger-happy! They've both put in for a transfer. I've heard them asking my dad to complain to your dad."

He has unnerved me and I'm silent for a moment. "That doesn't have anything to do with Moses," I murmur finally. "I just think it's unfair the way Miss Sadler treats him like a halfwit. And the way you guys make fun of his English. Besides, if that's the kind of home he comes from ..."

Robin loses patience. "He's not one of us and we don't have to be nice to him. Or to Danny. He isn't one of us either!"

This time I'm indignant. How can he be so callous! I want to rub his nose in his words like you rub a puppy's nose in the mess it's made on the carpet. But my challenge, when I blurt it out, rings hollow. His mother is right: I'm wishy-washy. "Whaddya mean by 'us'? Who are 'we' supposed to be?"

He looks away but is surely frowning. "I'll let you figure that one out for yourself. I know where I belong. See you 'round." He turns and stalks out.

The silence spreads in widening ripples. I look down at the cover of *Assignment in Space* and despair. There's no consolation from Boom-Boom's beaming pose either. I'll still be mulling all of this over next Monday when Robin comes back with more homework. We'll apologize and make up. Churchill is too small to be on the outs with people you have to deal with day to day. On the surface our relationship will become cordial again. But we'll both know that deeper down the divide between us hasn't been bridged. We stand on separate patches of ground. Mine may feel morally higher but his is definitely firmer.

Dave has reinstalled his mattress in the upper bunk. Tonight, when he climbs up into bed, I ask him what he thinks about Indians.

"Huh?"

"Like the ones you work with at The Bay."

"Oh, they're okay, I guess. We don't have a lot in common, besides hockey." Then he remembers my question. "What I don't like is the ones who go around hawking food they bought with their welfare stamps."

"Why would they wanna sell their food?"

"To buy booze, dummy. It pisses Dad off even more."

There's a pause as I turn this over in my mind. "What does white trash mean?"

"What?"

"White trash, what does it mean?"

"Where did you hear that?"

"On the radio. It was a program about settlers in the US."

"They were probably talking about poor southerners who went west to grab land."

"Why were they called white trash?"

"Because white people weren't supposed to be poor and landless like the negroes."

"That would make Grandpa and Grandma Haglund white trash. They came from the old country for free land and they were dirt poor. Mom says so."

Dave is annoyed by this. "They were homesteaders. They got about the last free land to be had in Manitoba. It wasn't much of a giveaway either. All it's good for is raising a few beef cattle. You've been there."

I picture the farm's stony pastures bordered by willows and sloughs. These I avoid because of the snakes. "Could you say there's white trash here in the north?"

Dave ponders this for a minute. "Not in that sense, because the government doesn't give away land. The guys who come up to open traplines can't own them. They're concessions. The only people I'd call white trash are the winos and misfits who can't hold down a job in the south, like old Balanchuck."

"Do you think they're any better than the Indians who sell their food to buy liquor?"

"They probably think they are. But I'm tired, go to sleep!"

I lie awake till past midnight. There's someone else who fits the description of northern white trash: Jeff's dad. I've smelled the alcohol that mists his eyes and trails him as he shuffles through the hall of the main school building. Once I watched him carry the slop-pail out of the girls' washroom, cursing and wiping his runny nose with the sleeve of his tattered sweater. 'Get outta my way afore I dunk your ugly mugs in this muck bucket!' he'd bawled at the Chipewyan kids clustered at the back entrance. He thinks he's better than them while in fact he's ashamed of his own inadequacy. He may have fought in Holland but he's a drunk and he's trash.

It's not hard to see where Jeff picked up his hostility towards Danny. Hostility that apparently rubbed off on Robin long before the clash over Nicky. I understand now why they banded against me. Sure, they're both a bit older and have known each other a year longer. But in a small town such differences tend to be overlooked. Or ought to be. Intellectually, Robin has a much closer affinity to me than he does to Jeff. So, the basis of their kindred spirit has to be the lowest of common denominators: Robin prefers scum of his own stripe to a half-Polack who keeps company with a half-breed.

I'll cling to this explanation until Robin leaves Churchill two summers from now, around the same time as Jeff. I like it because it discredits Jeff's and Robin's friendship while giving me cause to hold a grudge, just as Danny was given cause to hold a grudge by his conviction that the Mounties lied about Nicky. If I was less self-centred, I'd realize that there's more to Jeff and Robin being buddy-buddy than white supremacy. They probably joke more about girls when I'm not around. Jeff might even find me sanctimonious. Robin could simply be following his mother's guidance. In the new towns and cities where I'll live in coming years, the issue of not fitting in or wanting people to like me and being hurt when they don't will return to haunt me. I'll learn the hard way to live with such ghosts.

With Danny it's different. To begin with, unless he leaves Churchill someday, he won't have a decent chance to discover the bigger picture. The fate of Nicky will remain a chip on his shoulder, a colour-suppressing layer of recrimination that makes his world a collage of black and white images. Will he still be bearing a grudge against the Mounties in 2010, when the following CBC post appears on the internet?

Inuit dog killings no conspiracy: report[2]

The killing of Inuit sled dogs on Baffin Island more than fifty years ago was likely not the result of a federal government plan to force Inuit out of their traditional way of life, according to an Inuit commission.

The report by the Qikiqtani Truth Commission, released on Wednesday, provides a first-hand perspective on the dog killings and other major social changes Baffin Island Inuit faced between 1950 and 1975.

Inuit have long claimed that RCMP officers based in the eastern Arctic systematically killed thousands of their sled dogs – known in Inuktitut as qimmiit – as part of a government plan to force Inuit to abandon their traditional camps and move into

---

[2] Canadian Broadcasting Corporation news post dated 20 Oct. 2010.

western-style permanent communities.

'Between 1957 and 1975, the number of *qimmiit* declined dramatically,' the commission's report states in part.

'While some died from disease or were abandoned by their owners, hundreds were shot by the RCMP and other settlement authorities because *qallunaat* [non-Inuit] were afraid of loose dogs.'

Laws not properly explained

t has been alleged that about 20,000 sled dogs were killed from the 1950s through the 1970s in what is now Nunavut, the Nunavik region of northern Quebec, and the Nunatsiavut region of Labrador.

The RCMP concluded in 2006 that no organized dog slaughter had taken place. Some dogs were lawfully destroyed because they were diseased, starving or dangerous, according to the police force's own report.

I'll read this post by chance in the *International Herald Tribune*, on a train between Lausanne and Geneva. At first, I'll smile to myself, the kind of ironic smile you develop when you've lived abroad for thirty years with no intention of going back. Is this all they've got to write about over there, I'll ask myself? My stints as a child and young man in the north will be a scattering of vague recollections. I won't remember a thing about Robin and the stew I'm worked up into now, on my lower bunk in Churchill, or about Nicky and the blood on the snow the day before the blizzard. Yet a couple of phrases in the post will give me pause. The first one, '…force Inuit to abandon their traditional camps and move into western-style permanent communities', will draw a formless parallel to the morning last month when Janie recounted how sorely her parents missed their sled dogs and the trips to their winter fishing camp. Yet this will mean nothing to me because the memory of Janie will be blotted out, too, making the link a dead end—a bare wire hanging in empty space.

Then, just as I'm about to turn to other news, my gaze will be arrested again, this time by the word "starving" in the last line. Somewhere in space-time there will be a flicker, a ripple, and for a split-second a vision will surge in my mind of a scrawny dog, its coat colourless and patchy from malnutrition; it is sniffing and pawing at the charred debris that trail from an overturned trash barrel; it pays no attention as we drive by, staring uncomprehendingly at a rusty hubcap that blows past it like a tumbleweed; finally, giving up its half-hearted search in the rubbish, it presses its ears and tail tightly to its skeletal form and slinks like a blotchy paper cut-out into the driving snow.

How could I guess that this flash will have told it all?

The dog is the one that got away.

Cynthia

Churchill, May 1964

The Coke is a treat, the more so because this is my first visit to the Hudson Hotel dining room. All six arborite tables are occupied by men immersed in talk or card games. Some wear work clothes. Most puff on cigarettes, the geezers on pipes. I try to savour the atmosphere but can't help feeling an outsider as the only youngster in the place. I imagine myself the caribou head gazing in quiet meditation from the far wall, its antlers splayed like the upraised arms and hands of a priest delivering communion. I wasn't intended to hear the conversation between Dad and the stranger at our table. He has just arrived from the south, a feisty character with broad sideburns and a handlebar moustache. His son came with him for the train ride and the idea had been for me to show him around town while our fathers talked shop. But the kid, aged nine or so, took one look at our grubby backwater and muttered that he would rather stay in his hotel room. Submitting to a drink in our company, he downed his Dr Pepper in three long draws from the twin straws, avoiding eye contact with me, then stood up and left without a word, presumably to read his hoard of comics upstairs. His father apologized but in fact I'm relieved: there will be no need to chaperone a scowling city-slicker.

Dad is trying to keep the conversation cagey, so I turn aside and pretend to follow our neighbours' crib game instead. Actually, though, I'm cocking an ear to the stranger's steady spiel. While containing elements of self-flattery it's clearly backed by status that seldom reaches our remote corner of the world. He represents an adventurers' association with a cross-Canada membership and contacts in the States. Dad reiterates that their plan is still under wraps, but piecing together the snippets of information that fall in guarded tones, I surmise that the stranger is here to help set up a sport-whaling venture that Dad will head with government outfitting. The main purpose will be to provide work for idled Chipewyan hunters. Dad puts a finger to his lips when the talk turns to money, pointing out that they will get down to details later in the beer parlour. For the moment they're waiting to be joined by the bush pilot, who is to fly some of the sportsmen on fishing and hunting expeditions.

I presume the pilot will be Cynthia's dad and, sure enough, the room erupts in an exuberant welcome when he breezes in presently. I'm nevertheless surprised to see Cynthia's blond hair tossing behind him as they make their way to our table, pumping the outstretched hands and exchanging jovial greetings. My heat skips a beat: has she been invited for a drink as well? I've never noticed how short her father is, five foot five or six at most, with a slight frame to match. A good size to be boxed in a Beaver bursting with camping gear, he would joke. Dad wastes no time introducing him to the stranger and marches the two of them off to some earnest bargaining over pints of Molson's. Cynthia and I are left alone at the table. She's puzzled and somewhat annoyed.

"Where's his son?"

"You mean you were supposed to show him around too?"

"That's why I'm here."

"I think he's scared of getting eaten by a polar bear. He said he's gonna keep to his room till they leave town."

"Then we're both off the hook."

"Looks like it."

She thinks a second. "I was going to take him to the Eskimo Museum. My mom works there parttime and I help her on Saturdays…" More hesitation. "Have you ever been inside?"

I admit that I haven't though it's just down my street.

She makes up her mind: "Let's go, then. I'll show you a few exhibits."

By golly by gum! Is she asking me out on a date? Well not exactly, since her mother will be there. But still… "Uh, okay…" I mumble, trying not to sound too eager. Even as I pull on my jacket too hastily, inserting my right arm into the left sleeve. I can feel my cheeks redden but thankfully she's already heading for the door.

The adrenaline continues to course through my veins as I follow her out. Does this mean we'll be able to talk again? The fact is that Cynthia and I have hardly spoken since the Valentine's Day party at school three month ago, when she and I ended up Queen and King of Hearts. A word of explanation about this. A week before the party, in art class, everyone fashioned a Valentine's box out of cardboard, tissue paper and assorted decorations. The boxes bore our names and had a slit on top for Valentine's cards that could be slipped inside as a token of friendship or, more adventurously, of secret admiration. Miss Sadler laid out the boxes on the shelf beside Robin's and Roger's desks where she had a good view of them. They cheered her up, she confided. (It's rumoured she has a boyfriend in Selkirk whom she visited at Christmas.) The girls indulged her by oohing and aahing over the arrangement, which in my opinion resembled a graveyard with garish tombstones. Worse, after predictably starting as a popularity and beauty contest, the card-giving degenerating into the rank shenanigans and feuding of a frontier-style election. Jeff was warned and then disqualified for stuffing his own box in hopes of being paired as king with Wendy, just to crush her out, while Robin used his sleight of hand and Roger as a screen to remove cards from Danny's box (no one witnessed this except me and I didn't denounce it). Robin was just acting out of spite. As class jock he would normally have been assured an easy victory but the backlash from the Nicky drama proved fiercer than he'd reckoned with. Meanwhile, in the girls' camp it was a case of gerrymandering, with Yana and Carla expanding their sphere of influence to include Janie, who was nominally neutral, and thus outnumbering suck support from Sandra and Astrid for their champion. The upshot was that Cynthia and I, the most innocuous members of the class, ended up with the most cards when the boxes were opened and the contents revealed. Our reward consisted in donning paper crowns festooned with hearts and sitting at a small table laid out for us with Freshie and cake.

The embarrassment was devastating for both of us. Not that my crush on her was any secret but the Valentine's Day ritual made a humiliating spectacle of it. Nor has the ribbing abated much since, so I'm amazed she would offer me quality time in her company today. Has she decided it's time to shake off our discomposure? If so, I'm grateful. Fortunately, she finds something to say.

"This is the time of year I hate most."

I feel my tenseness easing already. "Why is that?"

"Because the winter keeps dragging on and on. They say there's another storm coming next week. Every time you think the snow will soon be gone we get more."

I survey the street. At the far end, set against the greyish snowbanks and greyer sky, the Catholic church gleams white as a beacon. It is easily the handsomest, and as it were, most spirited building in sight. Not that the houses we pass are all scruffy-looking. Some were painted recently and have shovels, brooms and other implements propped up neatly against their front porches. But others have never seen a paintbrush and are shoddily built, with tarpaper insulation flapping from their bare wooden frames. All are flanked by rusty water tanks, some by empty fuel drums and heaps of junk. The snowdrifts in front are discoloured from exhaust fumes and have dwindled to waist-high mounds, exposing litter and dog shit everywhere. The ice cover on the street is slashed by twin ruts down to the grimy roadbed. Thus the general appearance of the town is dreary, depressing even, and is set to get more dismal still. As the days grow longer and the temperature creeps up it will soon be rubber-boot season, with snowmelt forming ever larger pools that will turn to ugly sludge, unable to seep into the rock-like permafrost less than a foot below the surface.

Years from now, I'll read excerpts of a report by a government consultant sent here in the late sixties to evaluate the community's needs. He will be appalled by the 'unparalleled squalor' and lament that living conditions in Churchill are 'among the most wretched in Canada'. While that could be stretching it, if he comes at this time of year he can be forgiven for finding the place unsightly. The most urgent need, people will tell him, is for indoor plumbing.

"At least the fresh snow covers the garbage for a while," I offer lamely. Then I have an idea to keep the conversation going. "What's it like here in summer? We didn't come here till the end of August."

"It's better, as long as you can get away from the bugs," she allows. "The wildflowers brighten up the tundra. Rhododendrons, fireweed and so on."

"I saw berries before the snow came."

"You can pick buckets of cranberries and blueberries if you're patient. Sometimes I go out with Janie to gather berries and Labrador tea. My mom makes us drink it when we have a cold."

"So, you see Janie during the summer."

"She's about the only girl my age around." After perking up her tone has flattened again. "Everyone else goes south during the school break. We stay because that's when my dad has the most work..." She pauses. "...Though we probably couldn't afford a holiday anyway."

No one has ever confided in me this way and it makes me squirrely. I look sideways to scan her features, the first glance I've stolen since we left the hotel. She's not beautiful, that will come when she has fully bloomed several years from now. But her fine cheekbones and fair, gently curving eyebrows disarm me as always. I have to turn my gaze forward.

"The south isn't always that great. We'll probably spend part of the summer on my grandparents' farm, like every year. There's nobody my age either, except when my cousin visits for the day."

"Well, at least you get away. And you have your brother and sister."

I'm about to reply that she has a brother too when I remember he's only six and has Down syndrome. I find a new tack. "Dave promised to take me hunting partridges. He's got a .22 and says they're a cinch to shoot." A shadow crosses my mind. I stole the .22 last summer while Dave was in town and shot a bird that was perched peacefully on the telephone line. At first, I thought I'd missed it because it didn't move. But then, without a sound, it dropped like a stone and lay still on the ground, its wings drawn in tightly. I still hate myself. Why didn't I shoot a tin can instead?

"As long as you eat them…" she says. I struggle to remember what we were talking about but there's no need: she is still following her earlier train of thought. "What I really don't like is that nothing in this town is permanent."

"Whaddya mean?"

"It's not just in summer. Nobody stays here more than two or three years. Their fathers get posted here and then transferred to some other place. I bet that's what's gonna happen to you. Look at Wendy. She'll be gone as soon as school is over."

"For good?"

"Yes." Her bitterness is now unmistakable. "What's the point of making friends, among the white people anyway? They all move away sooner or later."

"Last year I had to leave my friends in the town where I was born. That was no fun for me either."

She thinks for a few seconds. "Okay, but if you go back in ten years they could still be there. Here you won't recognize anybody our age. Except me."

And Danny, I say to myself. So that's what's eating her. I've never thought about it the other way around. It's true that when Dad talks with other adults, they often refer to their posting, as if they've been pinned like a notice on a bulletin board. For as long as it's needed, until a new notice is put up.

I tell Cynthia that people leave Norton too. Two years ago, a couple of young guys cut the roof off their jalopy with an acetylene torch and announced they would drive it to the Calgary Stampede, with plans to stay and find work in Alberta or BC. The whole town turned out to see them off.

Cynthia is resolute. "I won't have a long-time friend to run away with. And anyway, girls don't have that kind of freedom."

We've reached La Verendrye Street. Dwarfed by the bell tower of the church next door, the Eskimo Museum cuts a low but modern profile highlighted by the gable-shaped canopy over the door in the middle. I ask Cynthia if it was built recently. She's glad to change the subject.

"About three years ago. The collection used to be stored in the Bishop's residence, but they ran out of room so Father Gilles raised money to create a proper museum."

"He's our scout leader," I tell her, surprised to learn that he has still other interests in addition to the priesthood. An incident I keep to myself is that once, while we were singing around the fake campfire on Scout Night in Caribou Hall, the bugger kicked me in the coccyx because my butt was sticking out from the circle. He may have just meant to nudge me but everyone knows he has little sympathy for Protestants. It takes us a lot longer to get promoted than the "mackerel snappers."

Inside, Cynthia's mom greets us and gives us slippers to replace our slush-covered boots. She is taller than her husband by a couple of inches, has straight, straw-coloured, shoulder-length hair and wears glasses that give her the appearance of a secretary or schoolteacher. Cynthia explains that the stranger's son wasn't interested in coming but that I'd like to look around.

"Then we'll give you a guided tour," her mother beams. I smile back and let myself be led to the large wall display featuring an array of traditional tools and weapons made of stone, bone, wood and walrus-tusk ivory. The nearby shelves are lined with small ivory carvings of birds, whales, seals, polar bears, kayaks and umiaks manned by paddlers, and a dog team and sled carved from a single walrus tusk. Cynthia picks up a fist-sized polar bear with great care and cradles it in front of me at eye level.

"This is my favourite piece."

The bear's flat head thrusts forward and upward from its long, sinewy neck. Its wide, rounded body is mounted on bulging legs and feet tipped with phalanxes of tapered claws. The impression is of sheer muscle and power accustomed to lording it over a forbidding land. I can't help shrinking back, for it looks set to lunge at me.

"Realistic, isn't it?" Cynthia's mother enthuses.

"And beautiful," Cynthia adds.

"It sure is," I reply to both of them. "Are they all by the same sculptor?"

"Oh no, the Oblate missionaries bring them from all over Keewatin when they come here for diocesan meetings."

I know from the radio that Keewatin is the section of the Northwest Territories that mainly comprises the islands north and east of Hudson Bay. I've memorized the names of the settlements from the weather report, which every morning gives the temperatures for Eskimo Point, Rankin Inlet, Baker Lake, Whale Cove, Chesterfield Inlet and Coral Harbour. It's still a lot colder up there than in Churchill. I inquire about the dark grey carvings exhibited on the other shelves.

"Those are soapstone. It's replacing ivory more and more. The artists find it softer and easier to work with."

The soapstone pieces are generally bigger. Besides the same animals and artifacts fashioned in walrus-tusk ivory, they include igloos and hooded hunters on slab plinths, sleds pulled by diminutive leather-harnessed dog teams, seal fishermen dangling hooks through breathing holes and other works. I marvel at the intricacy of the faces and clothing but there's something in the lines – a pureness – that I find even more compelling.

"These are for sale," Cynthia tells me, indicating the articles on the table by the counter. "The price tags are one of my jobs."

"Who buys this stuff?"

"Mostly government visitors and people from the base," her mother answers. "Sometimes officers from the ships that call in summer. A lot of Americans used to come souvenir hunting when they were stationed here. Our servicemen don't seem to have as much cash."

Back outside I ask Cynthia what oblate means. She looks at me questioningly at first but then remembers what her mother said.

"You mean the missionaries, the Oblates of Mary Immaculate. Father Gilles is one of them. He told us about the order in Catechism. The word basically means a sacrifice: they give their lives to the faith."

I ponder this. Trust the Catholics to bring Mary and her miraculous motherhood into the picture. But for all his faults, I can't help thinking of our Scout master with new-found respect.

"He tells me the names of things in French when he's here at the museum."

"You said nobody stays here permanently," I point out, believing I've spotted a flaw in her earlier preoccupation. "It sounds like Father Gilles and the other missionaries do just that."

Apparently, she has thought about this and has a ready rebuttal. "They chose to be permanent. I didn't."

Hours later as I climb into bed, shivering after the misery of my Saturday-night bath, the day's events continue to churn in my mind. Like the glass chips of a kaleidoscope, they break apart and come together again in new patterns with each rotation. I pull the blankets over my wet hair and lie face-up, mummy-style. When Sandy jumps up to nestle beside my pillow, I stick one hand out of my sarcophagus just far enough to stroke him.

The more I think about it, the more I'm convinced that the polar bear Cynthia held up to my face was no particular animal the carver wanted to replicate. It was too perfect. Besides, Cynthia's mother called the carvers artists, not craftsmen. Is that what art is about; creating things that are more than realistic? Truer than life? One day I'll read about Plato's realm of forms and will perhaps have a fleeting recollection that I can't put my finger on, a flash of the museum piece that for now is stamped on my brain like an icon. It floats in space – timeless, absolute, unchangeable – the artist's embodiment of an essence he was unconsciously striving to apprehend.

I'll see real polar bears during our time in Churchill. There won't be that many, two or three each year, and they will invariably cause a stir. Like the first one, which will lumber up from the beach a couple of months from now. It will scare the hell out of Mr. Panchenko, the federal caretaker, who will be perched on a ladder painting the post-office building next door. It will squeeze past him right up against our house and also scare the hell out of Mom, who will see it from the kitchen and alert Beth and me, who will be listening to records in the living room. I'll thus have a grand view of the animal just as it plods by the window, cool as you please. It won't remind me of the museum piece. It will be mean and hungry looking, with dim, sunken eyes and matted, yellowish fur hanging in folds from its hulking chest and sides. Following its nose, it will wheel left and head up the road to the garbage dump, possibly becoming one of the problems bears that will be shot in increasing numbers until an animal-welfare activist intervenes in the early seventies by raising money to have such bears anaesthetized and airlifted to an area well away from town. There, out on the tundra, they and their brethren will turn into a world-famous attraction observable by ecotourists from polar rovers.

Ecotourists will patronize the Eskimo Museum, rechristened the Itsanitaq Museum. Maybe one of them will fall in love with Cynthia and whisk her away to a new home, where she will never again regard transience with envy or as a betrayal. I hope that happens, or rather I will hope so once I've left Churchill and no longer have any claim on her, supposing I ever did. Right now, it hurts me that she should feel trapped. Though I find it hard to empathize with her plight, having no firm attachment to this town. I don't imagine myself a fixture the way I did in Norton. What I do feel is ambivalence about the whole setting, a rebus of conflicting emotions that I can't sort out yet but sense very deeply. It started on the train that brought us here last August. While so much else will be long forgotten when I write this, including Cynthia, her parents and Father Gilles, I will still be able to visualize that train because in 2000 I will again see part of it (or part of a sister train in the same series) conserved at the Winnipeg Children's Museum. I'll be amazed how clean and tidy it looks for a train that for decades will have hauled miners, trappers and hicks like me (though also ecotourists with fat bank accounts) through mosquito-infested woods and muskeg. Sadly, the dome car that I liked best won't be featured in the museum piece. Between card games and comic books, while Mom knitted, I would gaze out the panoramic windows. The views were awesome, fearsome, wearisome… In the first hours after leaving Norton, we seemed to be getting nowhere, pinned to the bald prairie like a flailing insect. The sky overhead was blue, still, infinite… Only beyond Dauphin did the flatness start to heave as we pierced the rocky bed of the Canadian Shield. The towns grew less frequent, as did the stands of oak and poplar, and a dark wall of spruce rose up on either side of the track. The forest formed a new never-ending sameness that gaped through the windows and threatened to swallow us up as we rolled ever further north. During the second night the train stopped and backed into Thompson. I woke up frightened, wondering if something was wrong and we'd turned back. Sleep came again at last, but fitfully, and I awoke sometime later to motionless silence. Terror seized me—we'd been shunted onto a siding at some desolate way station and abandoned there! I lay tense and shivering, waiting for something dreadful to happen. For an escaped convict, crazed by weeks of wandering aimlessly through the bush, to burst in with an axe and hack us all into chunky bits. But then the sleeping car lurched, protested with a loud groan, swayed and began rolling smoothly back in the direction we'd come. In the morning the black spruce had grown shorter and the sunlight noticeably more oblique. From the dome car we could sometimes see over the clubbed treetops and the spectacle was wondrous: a countless host of dwarf evergreens stretched on and on to the horizon. Again, it was as if we'd shrunk, this time to the size of a dust-mite creeping through a tangle of shag carpet—the taiga!. Westward it extended to Alaska and eastward to Labrador while north of us it gradually thinned out for another hundred and fifty miles to the tree line. But our direction was northeast, along the river, and in mid-afternoon the scraggly forest suddenly yielded to the mournful strip of tundra girdling Hudson Bay. There was a final squeal of brakes as we pulled up alongside the white, high-gabled station in Churchill.

There's a sound I associate with that first thousand-mile

journey: the falling pitch of the train's horn that trailed us as we trundled through the stillness of the night. Scratching Sandy's belly as I did while lying awake in the sleeping compartment, I can still hear the faint echo of that wail. And it will seem to echo again, or a sensation akin to it will, years from now when I read about others' first encounters with the Canadian wilds. Their vying fear and wonder will strike a chord and I will recall how those same conflicting emotions shaped the way I perceive the country I'm growing up in. The land is too big to bond with. The long wail of the horn was its solace. The train was struggling to requite the land's loneliness and suffuse its vastness. Without it the aching silence would have been for naught.

Night is falling. It often does well after I'm asleep now. In a month the rocks behind the house will be bathed in a red glow at midnight. But it will still be almost another month until breakup. One fine morning in July, the jumbled ice pack along the shore will have disappeared mysteriously overnight, pulled far out into the bay by the tide. The bear that lumbers by our house will probably have hitched a ride on one of the floes and swum a great distance to the beach. The *C.D. Howe* will clear a path through Hudson Strait for the first ships, led by an HBC supply boat. Belugas will dot the blue-grey offing. Once the ice still choking the river is flushed out by the current, they will teem into the estuary to mate. Dad's sport-whaling project will be able to get under way.

It will be marred by an incident and then a tragedy. The incident will be the loss of an outboard motor, improperly clamped on the backboard of one of the boats. The guides will spend their ample down time trawling with grappling hooks without ever recovering it. Swearing and fuming, Dad will dig in his heels and keep the venture rolling. One evening he'll even be able to joke about it over supper, telling us how one of the adventurers from the stranger's association was set up perfectly, right alongside a sleeping whale, and missed it. "He drove his bloody harpoon into the water! How he could miss a ton and a half of beluga twelve feet long is beyond belief!"

The drowning will cut the laughter short. I'll be at Danny's that day, admiring the glass ball he found on the beach while checking his fishing net. The RCMP paddy wagon will tear past the front steps where we'll be sitting and lurch to a stop down the road by the whale plant. Bart and Iver will jump out, run to the back and yank out gear including the same grappling hooks used to trawl for the outboard motor.

Dad will arrive soon in his blue Ford, followed by Robin's dad in the patrol car. They will survey the search operations gravely from behind sunglasses. Since Danny won't want to be anywhere near the Mounties, I'll join Dad alone and then watch from a respectful distance, overhearing Robin's dad as he questions a witness.

-"So, the guide fell overboard in a tight turn?"

"Looked that way."

"Was he standing in the boat?"

"Yes."

"Drunk?"

"Could be."

Dad will shake his head and curse under his breath, stubbing out his cigarette with the toe of his boot. The body will be found when I return to the scene in the evening. It will be brought to shore and left in the recovery boat to be examined by a doctor from the military hospital at Fort Churchill. I'll edge closer to the boat, drawn by morbid curiosity. Dad will notice and deter me: "You don't want to look in there. It's a dead man." I'll turn away, ashamed, but while they're conferring, I won't be able to help myself and will peek over the gunwale. He'll be lying on his side with his back towards me, a tangle of black hair spread over his oilskin collar. Thank God I won't see his face—I'd dream about it for sure! Though I'll dream about the slumped figure in any case. About his limbs flung lifelessly across on the ribbing of the boat. The image will evoke defeat, the downfall of an entire community. The drowning will be one of over fifty tragedies that befall the Churchill Band of Caribou-eater Chipewyan until they eventually return to their traditional way of life at Tadoule Lake, two hundred and fifty miles away. Rechristened, by themselves this time, as the Sayisi Dene, or People of the East, First Nation—a prouder name for a prouder band that survived on their own for at least fifteen hundred years and can do it again.

School resumes on Tuesday after the Victoria Day weekend. Cynthia and I revert to our earlier reserve but with an unspoken understanding, namely that she can trust me to keep her confidences. Who would I blab them to, anyway? Knowing a bit of what goes on in her mind doesn't make me feel privileged. Rather, I'm reassured knowing that she dwells on things the way I do.

Moses was absent from school part of last week and hasn't come back. When I inquire with Janie if he's sick, she looks away and says cryptically, "Ask your dad." Which I do at lunchtime. Dad hesitates, no doubt weighing the seriousness of the matter and whether it's within my range.

"I sent him to a residential school."

The words don't register until I suddenly remember that Dad is not only the Indian agent but also Justice of the Peace. He's speaking in that capacity now. But I still don't get it. "What for? What did he do?"

"He didn't do anything. It's for his own welfare," is all he will say.

As usual, I have to quiz Dave for details when he climbs up into his bunk. He didn't know Moses was in my class but confirms that Dad went to take him away last week, armed with a court order and accompanied by an interpreter, the two junior Mounties and a social worker.

"Any idea where they sent him?"

"Nope."

I recall what Robin said about Moses' father, that he's one of the worst drunks in Camp 10. "Was it because of his dad's drinking?"

"Dad said the charge was severe neglect. He didn't get anything to eat except the lunches at the church and what he and his brothers and sisters could scavenge at the dump. Sounds like their mother drinks heavily too. Now go to sleep, damn it!"

And as often happens I can't and picture the scene in Camp 10. Dad reading out the court order while the young Chipewyan interpreted consecutively. The father bent over in a corner, his face in his hands. Bart keeping a wary eye on him while Iver restrained the wailing mother. The social worker helping Moses pack his meagre belongings in a suitcase, then accompanying him in the paddy wagon to the airport. Like a criminal.

The term 'residential school' doesn't mean much to any of us yet. It sounds institutional, possibly comfortable. Clearly, for Moses the living conditions will be a big step up as they would be for a lot of kids in Camp 10 and the Flats too, for that matter. But as the country will one day find out, there is little guarantee that Moses' forcible removal from his home and community, such as they are, will improve his welfare. Will they shear off his hair? Will they strap him for speaking Dene until he forgets it altogether? Will they humiliate him in front of the class for his shyness? Will they lock him in a closet with no food for trying to run away? Will some pervert clergyman or attendant abuse him? Will he eventually come home broken, an alcoholic or a drug addict, having tried and failed to fit into white society? At the age of sixteen, in a new town back on the prairies, I'll have long hair and play in a band. Occasionally, we'll perform at dances in the gymnasium of the local Indian residential school. I won't remember much of Moses by then and in any case won't make a connection between what happened to him and that venue. Even so, when I write all this down so many years from now, it will please me to think that the soft-spoken boy I helped with math in grade five was among the bland-faced teenagers swaying on the floor of the gym – the guys on one side, the girls on the other – grooving in their quiet, undemonstrative manner to the swamp rock of Creedence Clearwater Revival.

Actually, running into Moses at one of those dances wouldn't be a great surprise: there are fewer than fifteen Indian residential schools across Manitoba. The real coincidences that the future holds in store for me will be more striking, like finding a thirty-year-old CP Air schedule left as a bookmark in my copy of James Joyce's *Ulysses*. And then there will be my serendipitous encounter twenty-five years from now with a man at a trading company in Geneva. The idea of him being who I think he is will be tantalizing—the kind of improbable improbability that life can deliver up only once, if that. As it will to Danny, the day he discovers the glass ball washed up on the beach. He'll know it's a fisherman's float, having heard of other such finds. But this one will be special, a real stray, as Andrew will conclude after examining it carefully. It must have been adrift for many years, given the heavy corrosion by sun, ice and salt resembling a layer of hoar frost. Moreover, water will slosh around inside, water that can't have entered through a crack but in infinitesimal quantities, possibly over decades, through tiny imperfections in the glass.

"You get those imperfections when you use recycled glass," Andrew will explain.

"Where's it from?" Danny will want to know.

"Well, we can't be a hundred percent sure, but…" Andrew will ponder, cradling the float in the palm of one hand while alternately rotating it and stroking his beard pensively with the other. "I knew an old guy in the Maritimes who'd lived all around the Pacific. His hobby was beachcombing and he had quite a collection of these floats in his boathouse."

"My grandfather has a glass ball with a model boat inside," I'll pipe up. "He says it's from Norway."

Andrew won't be listening. "He said most of them were Japanese. They get trapped in the currents and circle the Pacific for years and years. They drift northeast towards Alaska, then swing south with the California Current and get pushed west back into the North Equatorial Current, where the cycle starts over again. Occasionally a storm will blow a float north instead, over Alaska, and in that case, it's caught in an eastward current."

"That's the Northwest Passage," I'll remember from an SRA article on John Franklin. "Most of it is frozen all year. The float would just get stuck in the ice."

"If it gets stuck up in the polar ice pack it can move. This might sound crazy but once in a blue moon these things can cross the top of the world and end up in the North Atlantic."

"You mean…"

"Like I said, it's not entirely certain. See this button? That's where the glassblower sealed the hole he left with his blowpipe. If it wasn't so scratched and crusted, we might see his trademark embossed on it, with a Japanese character." Pause. "The best evidence is the colour. Look here where the glass was protected by the crisscross of the netting before it wore through and fell apart. You have a clear view of the green that was underneath. I saw a lot of that same shade in the old guy's collection. It's the colour of recycled sake bottles."

Part II

Thomas

Geneva, May 1989

"Mind your bishop," a voice cautions softly behind me. The hiss of the sibilant is familiar but I can't place it. Nor can I turn around to see who it is because obviously he doesn't want my opponent to know I'm being prompted. Concentrating on the chessboard set into the pavement in front of me, I zoom in on the danger: intent on castling, I cut off my white bishop's escape route with my king's knight. Alex, the fellow coffee trader who is playing against me, spotted the giveaway and has cleared the file ahead of his pawn at D7. With his next move (pawn to D5), my bishop's goose will be cooked! I can already picture Alex beaming and chuckling as he bangs the wooden pawn down into striking position. 'Pris comme un rat!' he'll gloat to the dozen or so bystanders chatting and munching on sandwiches near the park entrance, some watching the game idly. In our department, it's his phone that Alex slams down in triumph with the same exclamation. If his partner, Luc, isn't there to listen, he waits for the telex room to call, then dashes down to collect the trade confirmation and struts back to their office, waving the flimsy slip of paper under the nose of anyone he meets on the way, congratulating himself on having his counterparty over a barrel. I puff out my cheeks in feigned premeditation, stride forward to grip my knight and drag it to F2, freeing the bishop's diagonal.

Alex bites his lip and gives me a hard look. Soon, though, he's rubbing his chin and cocking his head craftily again, scanning the black and white squares for a new line of attack.

I wait a moment before shuffling to one side and glancing to see who my benefactor is. Thomas Roth, our maverick mailroom employee at Arlaud & Cie, is smoking a cigarette, staring off into space. I might've guessed! A man in his early sixties, he has wavy, wiry grey hair, a perpetually clean-shaven face and the sardonic expression of one who sees inanity all around him. When making the rounds with his mail trolley he occasionally stops by my desk to deliver an unsolicited opinion, usually a condemnation, on something or other. He's particularly unabashed when he finds me alone, having quickly profiled me as an extra-terrestrial visitor, like himself, to the one hundred and ninety-year-old trading company.

"Qu'est-ce qu'ils sont primaires, vous ne trouvez pas?" he sneered a few days after I began working for Arlaud. I turned to see him balefully surveying my colleagues through the glass partition that divides the office I share with my boss, Christoph, from the other glassed-in cages. Though taken aback by his contemptuous remark, which could be roughly translated as 'What a bunch of orangutans, don't you think?', I decided to humour him and followed his gaze over the alternating pairs of traders and assistants successively comprising the Arabica, Robusta and Cocoa Desks. They formed into two neat rows of heads extending to the far end of our floor. Christoph and I at the Non-Member Desk are the only pair with no adjoining assistants. We share one and a secretary with the Robusta Desk but handle most of the execution work and typing ourselves. As I'll find out later (from Thomas, of course) Lorenzo Bühler, head of the Coffee & Cocoa department, wants to keep our Non-Member business lean because it was, he who developed it and he still receives a cut of our profits. He has the corner office behind Christoph and me, where he holes up from two o'clock until after the close in New York at ten in the evening, chain-smoking in the dark with the glow of his twin monochrome screens casting an eerie halo around his pudgy face. In summer he rolls down the blinds to keep his office dimly lit. We call it the Morgue.

Until Thomas's snide remark that day in March, I'd never observed my colleagues carefully, absorbed as I was in my new job. Alex and Luc, at the adjacent Arabica Desk, as usual sat with their backs to me facing their assistants in the next office down the line. Because the partitions are amazingly sound-proof, they have to pound on the glass to get one another's attention and then either shout or communicate in sign language. As if taking his cue just as Thomas referred to the whole lot as "primaires", Luc beat on the window between him and Ralph, the ganglier of the Arabica assistants, and the two started gesticulating frantically, with Luc contorting his face to mouth words that Ralph was struggling to interpret. I nearly burst out laughing, for they indeed looked a bit like apes in a zoo. Beyond them, those of my colleagues in the other offices who weren't half-hidden by their monitors were almost all on the phone. The traders were leaning back in their swivel chairs, cradling the receiver between head and shoulder. Neither headset-microphone combos nor occupational therapists have been invented yet. Again, I sniggered to myself because the traders I could see all had uniformly bored expressions on their faces. Thomas noted my amusement.

"So, you agree." It was a prompt, not a question.

I thought for a moment. By this point in my career, I couldn't deny that the average commodity trader was driven by basic instincts. But what was average? I surprised myself by coming to the defence of the cocoa traders, the two I knew least.

"Well, Voide and Benson seem pretty articulate. Benson gives a course on commodity futures."

Thomas pooh-poohed this. "Benson might come across as sharp but he's got the wool over his eyes like the rest of them. The more they try and second-guess the markets the worse they get screwed. And his course is a primer for secretaries who think that if they sign up for it, the boys upstairs will be more interested in their brains than their knockers. They'd be better off learning about backwardation in private."

What makes Thomas's stream of sarcasm palatable is its well-aimed acerbity. And he has linguistic skills to match. He grew up in the Bernese Oberland so his native language is Swiss German. But he rarely makes a mistake in English, speaks fluent French as well and picked up tolerable Italian from a woman he lived with for some years. More striking still is his general knowledge. For a guy who never finished high school (they expelled him for rebellious behaviour, as I'll find out later), he can reel off in detail on a range of subjects, especially history.

The game with Alex in the Parc des Bastions soon turns into a rout. I haven't played serious chess for years, possibly not since my last summer in Prince George, BC, when my lubricious landlady taught me some novel moves. The fact is that lately, with the weather warming up, I was itching to get out of the office and accepted Alex's challenge as a chance to do so. At lunchtime Christoph often makes me stay alone with a sandwich while he plays tennis, in case Czechoslovakia is buying. Otherwise, I eat with Marcel, our young half-assistant from Annecy, and other colleagues at the cafeteria that Arlaud shares with a former banking affiliate. I dislike the clatter of cutlery though, and the talk about football doesn't interest me. Once, on the way to the cafeteria, I eyed Thomas walking alone ahead of us, twirling his umbrella expertly and whistling to himself. I envied his carefree manner.

After conceding defeat to Alex, who doesn't propose a return match, I head deeper into the park and find Thomas sitting on a bench in front of the Reformation Wall. He sees me coming but shifts his gaze just as I arrive.

"What do you make of the legs on that one, Mr. Swiantek?" He's ogling a passer-by who has shed her stockings to expose limbs left lily-white by the winter.

"When are you going to start calling me Ben?"

He pretends not to hear me. "Swiantek... That's Slavic."

"Polish."

"So, you're Catholic."

"No. My father was Catholic but we were brought up in the United Church."

"Is that like the Église réformée?"

"I suppose so."

"Then you should feel at home here," he makes a sweeping gesture towards the monument set into the wall of the old town. I study the four main figures, fifteen feet tall: bearded, dour-faced men in flowing robes, each clutching a bible. I recognize the names Calvin and Knox but not the other two.

"I had a professor at university who said Canadians' puritan streak stems from Calvinism and in Quebec from Jansenism."

Thomas muses a second and grasps the parallel. "Obsession with the original sin and predestination," he nods to himself. He's about to expound when I express puzzlement over the statue of Knox. Why should a Scot be represented in Geneva, I want to know? Thomas's eyes light up.

"Now there's an interesting character," he enthuses, seamlessly switching topics like a deft waiter changing my order. In ten minutes, Thomas tells me the complete story of John Knox, starting with the Reformer's involvement in the murder of a cardinal in Scotland. He not only knows all the dates but is also able to lace each episode with titillating anecdotes such as Knox's refusal, while a galley slave in France, to kiss a picture of the Virgin Mary. He threw it overboard instead, shouting, "Let her learn to swim!"

"Did he come to Geneva?" I ask, glancing at my watch.

Thomas reaches into the pocket of his suit jacket, pulls out a pack of Winstons, taps one out on the edge of the bench and lights it unhurriedly. Savouring the smoke and chuckling at Knox's irreverence, he explains how, while still in exile from Scotland but this time as a vicar preaching Protestantism to the English court, Knox had to flee to Geneva after Mary Tudor came to the throne. Here, seeing me fidget, Thomas pauses for a moment.

"Surely you've heard of Bloody Mary?"

I tell him I taught Canadian history in a past life but need to bone up on parallel events in Europe. He looks sceptical, no doubt aware that in the period we're talking about Canada had barely been discovered by the French. But it's time to go, I apologize. We clock in and out at Arlaud and I'm still in my three-month probationary period.

"Let's have lunch together sometime," I propose.

On my way back to the office I struggle to recollect something – anything at all – about the Reformation. Didn't I read somewhere that Knox was a misogynist? To my despair, those three years spent teaching history and geography, on an Indian reserve in northern Quebec, seem remote and inconsequential. Like the literature I studied at university. How singularly useless it all proved when I became a father and had to earn a proper living! The transition to an office existence has been humbling, the more so because all I can see for decades to come is a stultifying grind. As in my previous job with an importer, most of my new colleagues are pleasant enough and the coffee business can even be interesting. But despite those meagre consolations it's a rat race that leaves me little opportunity to read or think about much besides the shipping documents required to cash letters of credit. I long for the heady talk that filled my student days over cigarettes, beer and club sandwiches. Sometimes I fancy myself a former junkie who never really went straight and in the wrong company could wind up back on Boogie Street. Is Thomas the dealer who spotted me and lay in wait? Okay, he's an oddball and old enough to be my father. But so what? With him, at least, the talk is of the bigger picture.

In the staff entrance of Arlaud's six-storey flagship building, I turn the key in my punch clock and am annoyed to see that so far in May I've accumulated fourteen hours of overtime. A fat lot of good they'll do me, since the most we can carry forward to the next month is ten hours, which I already had before the end of March. The brass like to remind us in their monthly circular that a day has twenty-four hours. In truth it has more, I'd like to point out, but they're stolen from us.

Marcel flags me down with documents to be checked and signed. "The agent from Paraguay just called," he informs me. "He's coming for a meeting at three."

I gulp. "Ortiz?"

"Yes."

"Did you phone Christoph?" He's in Oman today, on a week-long tour of the Gulf States, visiting buyers.

"I tried but there was no answer."

Probably at the beach windsurfing. "Damn…" I sigh with irritation. "Did you tell Ortiz to come to the Dulara address?"

"Yes."

"All right, then. I'll meet him there. You take my calls from three to four."

It's just my rotten luck that Alejandro Ortiz should come to Geneva unannounced while the boss is away. My only previous contacts with him were a series of heated telex exchanges with his half-literate secretary a month ago. We had our fingers crossed because the lot he'd sold to us, fifty tonnes of Paraguay coffee for April shipment to Limassol, was delayed upriver from Asunción by heavy rains. That was the official version, Christoph explained to me. Actually, it wasn't Paraguay coffee at all: it was Brazil coffee re-bagged as Paraguay/Non-Member and they'd likely run into problems smuggling it to port. We were cheating on the International Coffee Agreement in order to get around Brazil's export quota and obtain a large discount for the importer in Cyprus. Lorenzo, our department head, had badgered us into using this gambit to boost sales. Christoph had been reluctant but finally gave in.

A word of explanation before I go any further. Ninety percent of our Non-Member business is above board. It consists in selling coffee and cardamom to countries in Eastern Europe, the Gulf and northern Africa that aren't part of the agreement to prop up coffee prices for the producers' benefit. But we also do some unsavoury deals, for example with our shipper in Kenya, and are boycotted by a couple of state purchasing agencies because of past misadventures. For slippery channels like these we operate under the name of a shell company: Dulara. It has its own letterhead, telex call sign and bank accounts and a postal address at the rear of our building. That's where Marcel has told

Ortiz to meet me at three o'clock.

The problem with some of these shady deals is that Christoph hasn't made it clear how secret the Dulara cover is. He always reminds me to avoid any mention of Arlaud when we work under the pseudonym. But depending on the client, he can treat the masquerade very lightly. Take the Syrians. My first involvement with them was in a tender for five hundred tonnes of Indonesian EK-1 Robusta. The sale, which I made myself at two hundred dollars a tonne, was thus worth a cool million! It was early in the morning and Christoph hadn't arrived yet. The telex room called to inform me that the Syrians' purchasing agency was asking to negotiate directly (the type of exchange that will one day be called an online chat) on the Dulara telex machine. The Syrian at the other end was rejecting our bid at two hundred and twenty dollars a tonne and proposing a counteroffer at one hundred and eighty. His manner was cold and ruthless. It reminded me of the blood-curdling tales one hears about Hafez al-Assad's jails. With trembling fingers, I managed to keep pace with his staccato bursts, apologizing that I was unable to accept and taking advantage of the previous day's market rally to prise his counter-offer upward. "You are right, sir, the ICA might not be renewed but there's still hope for a settlement. Yesterday's higher close is proof of that... I agree, Sir, but then again, the market has already been pricing in a possible collapse for months. It can't go much lower, even if that really happens..."
The upshot is that, while double-checking our calculation as I typed, based on the offer that we ourselves had firmly in hand from an agent in Singapore plus freight, insurance, certification costs, bank charges and a minimum three percent profit, I worked him up to what in any case had to be our final bid at two hundred. Trading is easy when you know these things cold. To my surprise,

the Syrian abruptly agreed to the price and signed off. When Christoph breezed in at nine o'clock, he immediately read the telex exchange, nodding with approval, and in a rare gesture praised my handling of the sale. When I replied with a rare slip into vulgarity that I was shitting bricks from start to finish, he laughed.

"They come across as attack dogs but that's just a show for their overseers. Actually, you couldn't imagine nicer people. I'll send you to Damascus someday to meet them."

"Suppose they find out I work for Arlaud? You told me they blacklisted us."

"They know perfectly well who we are. They're the ones who asked us to find a new identity after a quality dispute some years ago."

With Ortiz it's different on two counts. First, he's an independent agent and not a state entity. Second, I'm not at all so sure where we stand with him unofficially. Lorenzo met him on a tour of South America, laid the groundwork for the bogus Paraguay coffee trade and informed certain buyers, like the one in Cyprus, of what was involved. But Christoph, as I said, was a reluctant participant. The talks to renew the International Coffee Agreement (ICA) are rife with accusations of cheating, especially by Brazil, which at the same time is threatening to bring down the whole system if it doesn't get a larger share of export quotas. My guess is that Christoph is angry with Lorenzo for helping Brazil ride roughshod over the market. To safeguard his reputation, he has put me in charge of all communications with Ortiz, making it sound like I'm the boss of Dulara. I would have liked to clarify all this before seeing the agent this afternoon, but since that isn't possible, I'll have to muddle my way through the meeting. I'll start off by reminding Ortiz that he nearly missed the shipment date for our first deal. Then, insinuating that it was a test, I'll hold out the prospect of more business if our buyer in Cyprus is satisfied with the quality. Keeping the discussion on a serious note, I'll go on to talk about consumer tastes that I'm already familiar with in Lebanon, Malta and the other Non-Member countries around the Mediterranean. If he asks what our connection is with Arlaud, I'll be cagey at first and tell him we occupy the same building but are separate companies. If it's obvious he's wise to us, I'll switch to tongue-in-cheek mode, adding, 'Sort of like two peas in a pod, haha.' Maybe I'll even venture a sly wink, advising him never to do business with Arlaud as they can't be trusted, hahaha.

I've been waiting on the sidewalk for ten minutes when Ortiz arrives in a taxi. A lump rises in my throat as he climbs out: he has the build of a right tackle with natural padding. Worse, he looks confused and mad as a hornet. He glares down at me from his considerable height, refusing my outstretched hand. What's going on? The driver has never heard of our company.

Damn you Christoph! Damn you for being in Oman and buggering off to the beach! "Must be a recent immigrant," I mumble.

Ortiz is still fuming as I lead him into the dimly lit staff entrance. He inspects the rows of punch-clocks "Where's the receptionist? Where's Lorenzo? Are you trying to make a monkey out of me?"

God help me, another primate! I manage to compose my features while pressing my Dulara card into the hefty hand Ortiz is still withholding from me. He folds his fingers around it but continues to glower. "Come this way," I gesture towards the elevator, almost loath to turn my back to him. It's a long, wordless ride up to the executive floor with its soft lighting and plush carpeting. The visitors' lounges on the ground floor were occupied, so I had to reserve the HR lounge. The usher who gave me the key explained carefully which door it was. The other doors led to the offices of the top brass and I didn't want to walk in any of them, now, did I?

Whew—the key fits the lock! I turn it, pull down the handle and push the door. The green-gold wallpaper stirs my affective memory. It was here less than three months ago that Denis Arlaud himself, one of the two brothers who nominally head the firm, interviewed me. He insists on having the final say in hiring traders. I invite Ortiz to sit down in the chair I occupied then, and settle awkwardly into the larger chair opposite.

"Sorry I can't offer you a coffee. There's no room service on this floor, haha."

Ortiz remains silent, head bowed. I can feel my heart pounding in my chest, the way it did in primary school when a teacher put me on the spot with a question I wasn't prepared for. I was hoping the Paraguayan would be subdued by the opulence of our surroundings. I remember the spell that the mahogany furniture, Persian rug, ornate lamps and oil landscapes cast over me during my first visit here. What impresses me this time is the array of full-length portraits on the near wall. Having read up on the Arlaud family, I know now that the paintings represent the first six generations of the dynasty. I can't help admiring their unbroken procession through the vicissitudes of time. The first figure on the left, Emile, stands out in his late eighteenth century accoutrements: cravat, wig, hat and knee breeches. A descendant of Huguenot refugees from southwestern France, he married a local widow and founded a trading house with her inheritance. Their elder son continued to grow the company but the chief architects of its success were the third and fifth figures, whose synergies transformed the burgeoning group into a far-flung commercial empire. Emile's grandson Louis-Edouard, shown in tailcoat, double-breasted waistcoat and full-length trousers, established a banking arm to finance the firm's core trading operations while René, great-grandfather of the two brothers who are currently General Manager and Personnel Manager, bought the first cargo ship of what would become a small merchant fleet. René's grandson Cyril is still group chairman and was pointed out to me being bundled into the family limousine after a board meeting. I'll find out at the year-end Soft Commodities banquet that the guy is a doddering idiot. He'll tour the table to shake hands with each of us and will be well into his second round when someone has the gumption to say, "Well, hello again!"

I'm startled out of my reverie by a movement in the other chair. Ortiz's massive frame is squirming. His head is still bowed. He's toying with my business card distractedly, waiting for me to begin. "Well, now…" I stammer but break off. I remember the spiel I sketched out in my head earlier this afternoon but am unable to launch into it. The irony is too compelling. Here I am, a gullible prairie boy, cast in a con-game with a South American smuggler! In his country, he might be capable of putting out contracts on people who double-cross him. How can I have come face to face with such a character? As Thomas observes, I'm a tourist in this industry. But I've always been something of an actor as well, and today I'm determined to play the part. If farce is what they want, then farce it will be. And it will be entirely improvised. We're a financial company, I'll explain to the Paraguayan. That's the line Christoph once told me to use if I had to hoodwink someone with the Dulara cover. Now's the time! I clear my throat and begin my monologue while Ortiz peers at me warily from beneath his bushy eyebrows, not once interrupting.

Keeping the palms of my hands open to feign frankness, "Dulara has multiple holdings across various sectors and regions," I explain.. "The kind of outfit that has a finger in every pie, so to speak, haha. We occasionally deal in commodities as a side-line – rather seldom in softs like coffee and sugar, more often in oil and metals – but we're mainly geared towards sophisticated financial engineering for top-tier clients with money they want to put to work more intelligently than by parking it in term deposits, haha." There is no reaction from Ortiz. "We invest their assets across a very broad range of financial and non-financial instruments: equities, bonds, real estate, futures, hedge funds, funds of funds—even artworks for the really savvy types." I wink, again to no avail. Ortiz still won't bat a bushy eyebrow. "Now that may sound quite arcane but it all boils down to a simple principle: portfolio diversification. We play it safe by spreading risk across many different types of holdings. Like putting those eggs in many different baskets, haha…"

I've slowed down. My knowledge of investing has run out, rather sooner than I hoped, Ortiz stays silent for another long, uneasy moment. Keeping his head bowed, he turns my card over and over slowly in his huge mitts and nods to himself. Has he figured me out? Is he smarter than I give him credit for? Has he noticed that Dulara is an easy anagram of Arlaud? He frowns and looks up finally.

"Ben," he says, "Can I call you Ben?"

I'm flustered. "Sure, by all means. Call me Ben!" I babble, making it sound as if the suggestion has come from me.

"Do you like women?"

I stare at him uncomprehendingly. Have I heard him, right? If I have, it's no help. I don't know what to reply.

"…Well, I'm married…" I stutter, looking down at my feet.

"… If that's what you mean…"

"You look like the kind of guy who likes a good time."

"Um…" I can feel my cheeks burning.

"You should come to Asunción sometime. I'll take you out on the town and fix you up with two girls. Okay?"

"Uh…"

"Two!" He holds up a pair of meaty fingers.

Christoph

Geneva, July 1989

Christoph hasn't spoken for some time. He's stewing, his ample chin cupped in both hands, his elbows planted on the desktop running the length of the window that separates us from the Arabica Desk. It's best to stay out of his hair when he strikes this pose. The last time was after we lost the Tunisia tender. He sat there chewing his lip, as now, replaying each stage of the operation over and over in his mind, like the rounds of a lost prize fight. Everything had gone according to plan: our informant in Tunis had kept us posted on the other bids as they arrived; we'd waited until the last minute and undercut our lowest competitor. It always worked. Why not this time? "Are we a bunch of old women, or what?" he half shouted finally, pounding his fists on the desktop. God, how he could get worked up! The truth, we found out later, was that the purchasing commission decided to give the business to someone else to keep them in the game. Which threw Christoph into a deeper funk: games have rules that mustn't be fiddled with.

Today's game changer was no bolt out of the blue. It was more like writing on the wall that loomed and faded and loomed again until the characters suddenly coalesced into hard print overnight. I half expect Christoph to explode and rail against Brazil at any moment. Instead he simply shakes his head, bends over and starts fishing through the suspension files in the drawers between us. One by one he removes the current folders, stacks them on the desktop and, when he has the full set, begins reviewing the buyers, shippers, prices and terms of sale. I carry on with my work, occasionally glancing up at the overhead monitor. The fluorescent green grid of figures comprising the Arabica market has steadied. The rows of data on the back months in 1990 and 1991 haven't changed much for half an hour. And while the 'Last' fields for delivery in 1989 continue to light up every few seconds, signalling a trade, the spreads between the bid and ask prices have narrowed. The other traders whose faces I can see through the cascade of windows look uniformly worried, including Voide and Benson near the far end. Their cocoa market has fallen by half in the past four years and is threatened with the same coup de grâce that has just been dealt to the coffee market: the talks to renew the price-support agreement broke down irrevocably late yesterday. Alex, in the office next to ours, has his back turned but his face must be as tense as the others, judging by the shoulder muscles twitching under his short-sleeved shirt. Thomas opens our glass door to deposit a pile of mail and telexes on the desktop beside me. He can see that I'm observing Alex.

"I smell a rat," he smirks.

"New York just broke through a hundred," I tell him gravely. Before remembering that he often gets wind of things faster than we do. I'm about to ask if he has heard any fresh news on the other floors when Christoph frowns in our direction, intimating that he doesn't want to be disturbed. I get up and join Thomas in the aisle by his mail trolley. "It's a bloodbath," I shake my head, closing the door behind me.

"For some. In the end it's a zero-sum game."

"You say that because you haven't got any skin in it."

"I sure as hell don't," he chuckles wryly.

I tell him Christoph is checking our files for pitfalls.

"You guys play it straight. You should be okay." What he means is that at the Non-Member Desk we sell and cover, typically the same day, locking in our profit and leaving no loose ends. Lorenzo's orders. No hedging on the terminal markets and no long or short positions that might end up denting his take.

"Don't forget we sell to government agencies. If they back out of a deal, who's gonna take them to court?"

"True enough," Thomas concedes. "The Reds play fair, but you can never trust those greasy Arabs." A pause. "I suppose I shouldn't say that. Arabs aren't greasy, they're oily!" He smooths the shock of wiry grey hair on his forehead, visibly pleased with his brainwave. I have to laugh. "Anyway, your game is a lot safer than the one those morons play here in civilization." He gestures disparagingly towards the twin rows of traders and assistants manning the Arabica, Robusta and Cocoa Desks. They deal across Western Europe, i.e. in countries that are party to the international coffee and cocoa agreements. They regard the communist and Arab countries that Christoph and I cater to as backward and our back-to-back business model as stodgy. While envying our results.

"They're not allowed to be more than a hundred tonnes long," I point out and make a quick mental calculation. "The coffee market has come down thirty per cent in the past month. Supposing any of them were dumb enough to be long a hundred tonnes all that time, they'd be losing sixty thousand to seventy thousand dollars on paper. That's not a fortune. Dario can make that kind of money in a couple of months trading contracts." Dario is one of the Robusta traders who got fed up with the hassles of physical coffee and now only plays the futures market in London.

"That's if they follow the rules." Thomas releases the brake of his trolley and rolls it forward.

When I join Christoph again, he's still leafing through the stack of files with a wrinkled brow. They range in size from nearly empty, where the lot has so far simply been bought and sold for forward shipment, to folders bulging with copies of the bills of lading, quality certificates, letters of credit, invoices and telex exchanges. In these deals we've probably already cashed the shipping documents and delivered the coffee, so we're either waiting to be sure it's safe to pay the shipper or biding our time to earn credit interest.

This loathness to pay up bothers me. It's part of the top-down disregard for producers that rankles my Peruvian neighbour, Ademir, even more. He and I have children the same age and agree on most things. Moreover, we like speaking Spanish together. But he's homesick for Peru, which can make him surly and wont to call me a capitalist swine for working as a commodity trader. He can't forget the plantation workers he saw once, waiting in the rain at sunup to find out whether they'd have work that day. The 'lucky' were picked one by one and herded into the back of a pickup while the others trudged home barefoot. What I'd like to tell Ademir but don't have the courage to do so, is that coffee growers are eager to sell to an upright middleman like Arlaud, whose word is its bond. They wouldn't dare to deal directly with our customers and vice versa, so in fact we're doing both sides a favour. Still, in my mind our position is tenuous. How long will it be until our buyers, in their crumbling offices from Warsaw to Casablanca, start following FOB prices on their own monitors? Or until our shippers start using documentary credits confirmed by a reputable bank?

Behind us, Lorenzo opens the door of his office just wide enough to poke his bald head through. He exchanges words in Swiss German with Christoph, who swears under his breath when we're alone again. "The old fart wants to see us in half an hour," he groans. "About the big, executive decisions they made this morning."

I know why Christoph is ticked off: he'd planned to leave early to go watch his son play football. Now, perhaps as bad, he'll have to put up with the smell of cigarette smoke that permeates every inch of Lorenzo's office. Just thinking about it gives him a headache.

I'm puzzled that Lorenzo has included me in the meeting. He usually informs Christoph on strategic moves in private so they can jabber in Swiss German. Sometimes I kick myself for not learning German when I had the chance. The only opportunities I have to use Spanish are with secretaries in Costa Rica and Nicaragua. The outfit in Guatemala is run by German Swiss and Germans (possibly the sons of escaped Nazis). And that's just the tip of the iceberg. When I reserve dollars at Arlaud, it's from a German Swiss currency trader in the Finance department. When I need details on a freight forwarder in Malaysia, I phone a German Swiss colleague at our office in Kuala Lumpur. The whole chain of command above me in Geneva is German Swiss, from Christoph to Lorenzo to the head of Soft Commodities, Rolf Gasser, to the Deputy General Manager, Luca Wernli. I asked Thomas why the company is overrun with Totos.

"The French are nincompoops at languages and that's what trading is all about. Besides, nobody understands dialect or wants to learn it so that can be useful. Same with Dutch."

I couldn't resist a jibe. "Don't you feel like kids speaking Pig Latin?"

"Dialect might seem an ugly anachronism to you, but that's because you don't know our history." A mischievous smile crossed his face. "Did you like it when De Gaulle said 'Vive le Québec libre!'?"

"What's that got to do with it?"

"It was probably the last time you had something shoved down your throat by a foreigner." He paused and baffled me again by switching back to the original subject: "Actually, we do feel like kids in the schoolyard, before going into class. There's a kind of freedom in speaking dialect."

I'd never thought of language as a political weapon. As for De Gaulle, I've since remembered how furious I was at the time. We should have boarded the asshole's ship in the Saint Lawrence and strung him up from the radar beacon.

Lorenzo stubs out his cigarette as we walk into his office. Although he leaves a window open in summer, there's little ventilation because of the drawn blinds. I'll be monitoring a headache myself by the time this is over, I think irritably. I seldom come here. The first time was on my induction day, when Lorenzo lectured me on Arlaud's time-honoured reputation that he was counting on me to live up to. Pushing his overflowing ashtray aside, he invites us to pull up chairs without looking at either of us. Instead, he gazes over his clasped hands at a point on his desktop as if meditating. It occurs to me that he has never looked me straight in the face. With his squat stature, short neck, bulbous eyes and horn-rimmed glasses, he resembles an owl peering down from a tree branch. More self-important than wise.

"I was upstairs with Rolf and Luca all morning," he begins. "Jarvis called from London at midnight to tell me they tore up the agreement."

"For now," Christoph breaks in, hoping to air his well-stewed take on the collapse. "But when Brazil comes crawling back…"

"They won't!" Lorenzo barks. He's clearly intent on sticking to his agenda. "They're gambling they can sell all the coffee they want in a free market."

"At starvation prices," Christoph nearly pouts. "They'll ruin it for everybody."

"Not for us," Lorenzo straightens his short back. Here we go with the directives he carried down from the mount. "First things first: we're renaming your desk. With no more quotas, members and non-members, from now on you'll be called EEMA for Eastern Europe/Middle East/Africa."

"Philip Morris has a division by that name," I quip, unsure if I'm being supportive or cheeky.

Lorenzo stifles me with an impatient wave of his hand. "More to the point, you'll have to do more volume. Like Brazil, to compensate for the drop in prices. We've decided to go after a new market…" He pauses for rhetorical effect and raises his eyes for the first time. They're shining. "… Algeria!"

"Scheisse!" Christoph hisses through clenched teeth, slapping his forehead.

Lorenzo must have been expecting a challenge. Unruffled, he concedes only an owlish blink. "You…" he now looks squarely at Christoph, "…on the sell side. And Ben…" he shifts his gaze in my direction without quite meeting mine, "…on the buy side. Here's how it works…"

Christoph has covered his face with both hands.

I know I shouldn't be leaking the plan to Thomas but can't help sounding him out the next day in the park. Since our first encounter in May, we've been meeting once a week for a sandwich on the same bench facing the Reformers. Sometimes I imagine him as a kind of Socrates mentoring me under the stare of marble statues in the Forum. On the face of it, I've become more than an audience for him to spout off to. An attachment has grown between us that defies his natural antagonism and tempers my reserve regarding our age difference. Not that this budding friendship has excused me for being an ignorant colonial, as he reminded me early on when trying to explain the notion of combourgeoisie, in reference to the Bernese coat of arms at the base of the monument to the Reformation. "Sounds like an alliance to me," I shrugged. While keen to learn about the construction of the Swiss confederacy in the Middle Ages, I'm still struggling with the jigsaw puzzle of Europe's monarchies, wars and treaties.

Thomas listens to my recap of the meeting with Lorenzo and Christoph's hapless objection to going for Algeria. "If they're as dirty in business as they are in politics, I'd want to steer clear of them too," he observes. "They've been double-dealing for generations. Look how the students got tricked into rioting last autumn."

His recall of events is astounding. I vaguely remember reading about Algeria's Octobre Noir at my old job, when I had time to open a newspaper. "It wasn't anywhere near as bad as Tiananmen," I counter. "Seems to me the government even promised a new constitution and multi-party elections…"

"And in the meantime, they're torturing thousands in the jails. They aren't any closer to democracy now than they were under the French, helping massacre their own people."

I've heard enough. "Eastern Europe is moving towards democracy these days."

"Some countries faster than others." Thomas removes a bit of fat from the ham protruding from his sandwich and tosses it to the trio of sparrows watching us. They race in and squabble until one makes off with the prize. The other two edge closer. "You ought to be proud of your Polish relatives. Which part did your ancestors come from?"

"Galicia. They left before the First World War."

"Then there was no Poland for them to leave behind, only occupied territories. But they were better off under the Austrians than in the other two partitions." He takes a swig of beer and wipes his mouth with the back of his hand. "Talk about having German shoved down your throat—the ones who were colonized by the Prussians knew what a yoke is."

"Didn't they revolt a couple of times?"

"A couple of times!" The way his face brightens, I can tell I've hit on a pet subject. "Between the end of the Polish-Lithuanian Commonwealth and the Spring of Nations, there were half a dozen uprisings. The one in 1846 was the most compelling because it was coordinated across all three partitions. By groups meeting in secret, like Solidarity did when it was still underground."

"1846, that was during the Irish potato famine," I recall, pleased to bring up a pet subject of my own. "The Irish went to Canada in droves. They were losers, like the other early settlers: the French, the Loyalists, the Scots who got kicked off their land... And the Indians, of course, the first settlers and biggest losers of them all! Losing is embedded in the Canadian psyche."

Thomas doesn't bite. "People were hungry all over Europe. Tenant farmers couldn't make money any more as craftsmen because of manufacturing. So, they joined the liberals, the socialists, the republicans and the nationalists—everyone who had a beef about land or power."

"Do you think the Soviets will put down the movement in Poland?"

He exhales a cloud of blue smoke from the cigarette he has just lit. "They would've crushed it long ago if that was their intention. The USSR is turning inward. They're pulling their troops out of Czechoslovakia and Hungary. If you watched the news the other night, you'd know that Gorbachev told the Warsaw Pact to choose their own roads to socialism."

"I heard it on the radio." And could scarcely believe my ears. Gorbachev is so unlike the stone-faced Kremlin scarecrows we've always known. How could such a congenial fellow have risen to power in that murderous inner circle? What a shame the Russian people will soon despise him! "So, you think what's going on in Poland is part of something bigger."

Thomas doesn't hesitate. "Hungary will be next. A quarter of a million turned out for the reburial of Nagy last month."

"Nagy?"

"Imre Nagy, prime minister of the revolutionary government in 1956. You were still wet behind the ears, but I can remember the trainloads of refugees coming through Bern. They weren't losers. They were ordinary people ahead of their time."

Back at Arlaud I nip into the telex room to see if there are any answers to the inquiries I sent out this morning. All three telex operators are hunched over their keyboards, copying messages. These arrive from the upper floors rolled up inside capsules, which pop out of the pneumatic pipeline running through the centre of the building. Futuristic, I thought, the first time I observed the system in action. Now it seems archaic, like our ageing mechanical typewriters that clang and clatter as we churn out trade confirmations and long-winded instructions on how to word letters of credit. These are the kinds of message, each composed from scratch, which the telex operators are dutifully copying. Although the whole process reeks of redundancy, our eyes won't be opened to the scale of it until the deeper penetration of faxes and the advent of e-mail. To my surprise, the normally stingy and tech-shy brass in May bought a commodity trading program called Icarus, (I swear that's the name!) to obtain a comprehensive view of business development. As a consequence, each department is now equipped with a computer terminal where we punch in data on each new purchase or sale, which is then assigned a number by the program. We're anxious to see who will win the bottle of champagne that's waiting for the trader who enters contract number 1000.

Christoph hasn't come back from lunch when I return to the office. Still sulking after yesterday's rebuff, I bet. He didn't say a word all morning. It's true that we'll be out on a limb if we win the Algeria contract. According to the advance notice issued by the agency the government has appointed, the tender in September will be for 2500 tonnes of Indonesia EK-1, five times the quantity I sold to Syria. Even though it will be the lowest-grade crap available in a market down by a third, the deal will be worth almost three million dollars. To fill an order that size, I'll have to tap at least three shippers and charter at least one container ship for us alone. Christoph is to coordinate the sale with an operator in Paris who has spent years wearing out the seat of his pants in the antechambers of the Algerians' ever-changing agencies. He has been itching to work with Arlaud for some time and recently assured Rolf and Lorenzo that for a stiff commission he could grease the right wheels. All we have to do, he said, is swing the rock-bottom price the Algerians are prepared to fork out. And the market rout may have brought that level within reach.

Yet there's more to it than being overstretched: Christoph is afraid we'll be walking into a trap. He plays tennis with a trader at Plymouth, who won the last Algeria tender three years ago. They paid the right people to get the nod, only to lose their entire profit and more over a quality issue. It couldn't be settled by arbitration (the normal procedure), because Plymouth had instead had to sign a performance bond allowing part of the payment to be withheld indefinitely if the coffee was deemed unsatisfactory.

"No offers yet," I announce when Christoph finally stalks in without a greeting, well after two o'clock. "Still mad at Lorenzo?"

'You're forgetting who's boss,' his look tells me. He rolls a blank message slip into the carriage of his typewriter and starts hammering the keys. I go back to daydreaming with folded arms. There's nothing to do. New York hasn't opened yet but will no doubt be as listless as London. Growers, roasters and the trade have all backed off since yesterday's plunge, leaving only speculators to sniff like wolves through ruins after a medieval sacking. Physical business was already dwindling in recent weeks and has now pretty much dried up. The only inquiry today was from our buyer in Beirut, who is out of touch half the time anyway, owing to power cuts. The telex he sent this morning ended as they often do: "The bombardments are starting again. We are leaving for the shelter. Please pray for us!" I shudder to think what his rocket-pounded neighbourhood might resemble after fourteen years of civil war.

Christoph tears the message out of his typewriter, scans it rapidly and pushes his chair back. He's about to stand up and march out to the tube portal, head bowed as always, when he notices me staring into space.

"Haven't you got any work?"

"Nope."

"Have you looked hard?"

I turn to face him. "Even Icarus is up to date." This is meant as a barb after the three Saturday mornings I've spent feeding data into the trading program. With no champagne to show for it.

Christoph nods and sits back. My remark is registered. Despite working side by side for five months now, we've never hashed out the issues of unpaid overtime and minding the phone at lunchtime. I know he appreciates me, especially for my autonomy, though he has never said so. I heard it from the leggy blond secretary we call Barbie. She also told me I was hired to replace a guy with an MBA who came to work in a suit and drove Christoph mad because he couldn't compose a telex. Christoph didn't want another university graduate but that's the new profile the brass has set for traders: educated, preferably married with children. Men (this is still no place for a woman) who won't make rash decisions. I study Christoph's broad, fleshy face. Something has changed since the market crash and Lorenzo's refusal to heed his warning. Is that a glimmer of pathos beneath the hard-set features? A different face peering out from behind bars? If so, does he realize he has built his own prison? He can't talk to the other traders, who resent him for complaining openly about their losses at staff meetings. Nor can he talk to his buddies at the tennis club, where he cultivates the image of a rugged warrior. He has no one but me, his junior in age and rank, to open up to.

"Look at that Schlammassel!" he points in disgust at the monitor. "Coffee and the dollar are worth bugger all! How are we supposed to make money?"

"According to Lorenzo, by doing more volume."

His lip curls. "He's in it for his commission, with that mucker in Paris. They don't give two hoots about how much the Algerians are gonna soak us for!"

Without letting on that I blabbed to Thomas, I pick up on a strand of our conversation in the park. "Why don't we go after new markets in Eastern Europe instead? Like Romania and Bulgaria? Thomas says that if push comes to shove, their regimes will hang on the longest."

"Thomas is full of big ideas!" Christoph storms. "What does he really know about those countries? Algeria at least has oil revenues, even with prices dropping. Romania hasn't got two nickels to rub together! Any deals with them would have to be triangular, by finding someone to buy their pork. That's all they produce and most of it already goes to export. The locals get the innards and whatever else they can scrape off the floor of the abattoir. With Bulgaria we'd have to find someone to buy their electronics without getting into a lawsuit. The stuff is made with stolen technology."

"We've got a whole department on the fourth floor devoted to triangular business."

"They can't make pigs fly. There's not enough markup on coffee to make it worth their while." A pause. "Eastern Europe has always been a tough nut to crack. We used to sell to Poland but now they're buried in debt. Hungary and Yugoslavia could soon go that way too. You must have seen that Kospol is our only regular buyer, besides Albania, and that's because the Czechs care about their credit rating. If they started denationalizing and we had to sell to private roasters, we wouldn't know who we were dealing with or if they were solvent."

"So, you are worried about what's happening."

"Of course, I am, and you should be too." All of a sudden,

he's earnest. "Just tell me one thing, Ben."

"What's that?"

"Does this work interest you?"

Somehow, I was ready for this question and don't hesitate: "Yeah, I like this job. Wouldn't be here otherwise."

He eyes me warily. "I hope that's true… 'cause I'll need you. Things are bound to get worse around here before they get better." He stands up, rolls his message around a finger and marches out to shoot it down the tube.

Thibaud

Geneva, October 1989

Love is blind. I fell into coffee's arms at the import firm where I worked previously. The lousy pay and menial tasks (like tallying up warehouse stocks and tidying the kitchen) ought to have put me off. But it was a relief to be in employment again after a stint on the dole, and two aspects of the coffee trade first intrigued and then enraptured me. One that I sorely miss at Arlaud, where we wheel and deal in far larger lots but never see the underlying goods, was hands-on experience with raw beans. A sensuous new world opened up as I learned to screen them, count their defects and recognize their origin: by colour, from pale natural Brazil to deep-green washed Colombia; by shape, from flat, pan-like Kenya beans to their round Ethiopian cousins; and by size, from giant, bleached Malabar to the beady, drab Robustas of Cameroon, Ivory Coast and Zaire. Best of all, with three small roasting machines in the kitchen I prepared weekly tasting sessions, where my boss Thibaud and I would cup the samples we received from shippers. After sniffing each spoonful sedulously, we would slurp it, roll it around our tongues and palates and spit it out with a nod or a terse comment before moving on to the next cup. Two years into the job I was able to identify many provenances blind and even distinguish between certain neighbouring countries, such as full-bodied, fruity Costa

Rica and spicy, velvety Guatemala. It grieved me that coffee, with all its subtleties, had never achieved the stature of wine. In my mind Yirgacheffe Kochere, with its floral aroma, bright acidity and sweet, silky mouthfeel, was every bit as noble as a fine Burgundy. For rarity, Jamaica Blue Mountain was a gem on par with a prized Côte Rôtie.

The other part of the business that carried me away was trading. It was a mystery I longed to unveil, like a beauty heard of in legend. Thibaud chafed at my impatience. "You want me to teach you in a couple of months what it's taken me twenty years to work out," he chided me in his sly, taunting manner. Just my luck—a hoarder of trade secrets, I'd grumbled to myself. Until someone told me he'd never had an educated assistant before, only young deadbeats he hadn't bothered to train. The real problem was that he'd grown used to running a one-man show. So, I'd continued to pepper him with questions until late one afternoon, it was he who relented and agreed to spend a few moments each morning exploring a facet of price formation.

I left work that day excited and during the night had a dream that I now know was a portent. I was wandering through a dark, dank passageway, possibly in the bowels of a castle given the medieval weapons and armour adorning the walls. Drawn by the odd sounds and a shaft of light issuing from behind a door that was ajar, I pushed it open and found myself in an ancient laboratory. In the centre stood a high bench, lined with beakers and flasks and flanked by an array of tanks, vats, pipes and condensers that puffed and hissed. Behind the bench, Thibaud was transferring bubbly liquids from one flask to another, his face shrouded by clouds of steam. He uttered words I couldn't distinguish for the noise and seemed oblivious to my presence. When the steam dissipated for a moment, I realized why: his eyes were blank.

Truth told, my early impression of Thibaud was of a hermit sorcerer. And while time would erase the magic I read into his methods, I still remember him as a solitary eccentric. He certainly acted and even dressed the part, with those red trousers and two-tone oxfords he wore day in and day out. From what I gathered he had no social life. A hardened bachelor, he lived with his widowed father who accompanied him on holidays, skiing in winter and fishing in summer. Colleagues whispered that Thibaud was gay, and if so, I suspect he was a closet homosexual. He never made a move on me. Though seemingly aloof at first, absorbed for hours on end in his calculations, he became surprisingly good company after noting my growing interest in cupping. When prompted he could even be loquacious, with awkward bursts of jocularity. He had a bushy beard that he would smooth whenever he laughed, often to himself. I liked to observe his morning rituals. After stopping at the coffee machine with a newspaper tucked under one arm, he would breeze into our office at nine or so, smelling of pipe smoke and a liberal dose of cologne. Greeting me with an avuncular pat on the shoulder as he made his way to the other side of the desk facing mine, he would sit down too heavily and spill a few drops of his coffee, which he then proceeded to sop up with a handkerchief soiled by other spills.

"I see you're scouting bright and early," he would comment wryly with a mock growl, watching me pore over the telex circulars with lists of offers we received from shippers and other trading outfits. By this time each morning I'd already studied the previous day's close of the New York exchange, calculated its relative strength index and read the market reports on our news feed, including the one by Bob Jarvis at Arlaud's Manhattan office. "So, which way are they coming at us today?" Thibaud would ask with a conspiratorial wink while dropping half a lump of sugar into his coffee.

This was my cue to question him about something I'd noted or wanted to develop further. He would listen to my queries in rapt silence, nodding to himself, and then stir his coffee intently counter-clockwise as if to tease out his answer. It took me a while to understand that I was tapping knowledge he'd gained through empirical observation, knowledge buried in a deeper level of cognition. When he furrowed his brow and slowed the backward rotation of the spoon in his cup, it was because I'd hit on a topic he'd never consciously thought about. The upshot is that I extracted the components of pricing one by one like pages from Thibaud's grimoire. They formed into three categories. The constant factors – incoterms, freight rates, insurance and the like – had to be learned by rote. Differentials, or the premiums and discounts on the various origins and grades, moved seasonally and in response to demand, though often in established ranges. These could also be retained to a point. Random developments, such as weather, diseases, crop size and other local variables, could be gleaned from the market reports I was already hooked on.

I compiled a hefty list of rates and differentials and committed them to memory. By further factoring in the day's futures prices and exchange rates for lots offered in Swiss francs, it became possible to make sense of the offers we received from shippers and other trading firms. In essence, pricing was an onion that one had to peel through in search of underlying value. The exercise captivated me and I mastered it sooner than it took me to recognize the chocolaty notes of roasted Honduras blind. What really held me in thrall, though, was the daily dance of coffee prices. I pictured them as figures within figures of a grand yet intricate choreography, swaying to strains that only insiders could hear: a tou1ch of frost in Mongiana; rebels blocking exports on the road to Douala; the latest auction in Nairobi; a rumour of price supports wavering in London.

If pricing had baffled me at first, Thibaud's trading strategy remained even more of a conundrum. I knew his obsession with staying balanced (market neutral, it's called), but he never bought the same type of coffee that he sold or vice versa. He relied instead on an elaborate replacements system he'd developed over the years.

"It's my own invention," he told me proudly during a question-and-answer session, speeding up the backward rotation of the spoon in his coffee.

"Can you explain it?"

He puffed out his cheeks and thought a moment. "I'll give you an example. This morning I sold 200 bags of Guatemala hard bean ex-warehouse to Villars. We settled on 3.60 francs a kilo."

I made a quick mental calculation. "That's equivalent to the shipper's price from origin today plus freight and insurance."

"Good lad!" He stroked his beard, pleased with the results of his tutoring.

"So, where's the profit?"

His eyes shone. "In the replacement!" He took a sip of his coffee and set the cup down with a clatter. "There's no point buying a new lot of Guatemala, we can't get it any cheaper ourselves. I think I'll order a container of Minas Gerais from Carmo for March shipment at $1.13 FOB."

I'd seen the offer. "That's twelve cents below the benchmark."

He was beaming. "We should be able to sell it at minus eight cents this summer."

"And what if there weren't any bargains today? I know you never stay short."

"Then we'd buy a spot contract," he said confidently, "and sell it when we can get Guatemala at a lower premium."

That, in a nutshell, was Thibaud's system. I felt betrayed at finding none of the wizardry I'd imagined in it. Perhaps because of my dream about the laboratory, it reminded me of a book I'd read about medieval medicine: the remedies kept calling for dragon's blood, and since no one could find a dragon, the writer allowed all manner of common ingredients as substitutes. Over time, I began to doubt the system's originality as well. Judging by the price circulars we received from other players in what we call 'the trade', everyone must have adopted a similar gambit. We were all selling at market level because of oversupply, so the only way to make money was on the buy side, by squeezing shippers and competitors desperate for a sale. Roasters in turn squeezed the trade, playing us off against one another. Those that Thibaud regarded almost as friends were the ones who leaned on us most heavily. It was no mystery why they kept coming back: more often than not, he caved in.

The market grew tighter as time wore on. The fiercer the competition, the deeper Thibaud withdrew into his abstruse calculations. He had a ledger that he would take home in the evening and pore over each day, scribbling in the margins and connecting entries with arrows that fanned out in all directions. One day after fiddling in his ledger for an hour after selling fifty bags of Salvador, he slapped down his pencil.

"It's all I can do managing physical coffee," he spouted. "I want you to take over the futures contracts."

The prospect pleased me, the more so as our overall position was growing. I liked calling the broker with our order, watching for it to come up on the screen when it was transmitted to a jobber in New York or London and seeing it flash in the "Last" column when the trade was sealed. But the mission wasn't all fun and games. If there was no execution yet when I left work in the evening, I would come back anxious the next morning, praying that the market hadn't taken off in the opposite direction. What really began worrying me, however, were the roll-overs. These came in the last days of trading in the spot contract before it disappeared and was replaced by the contract on the first forward month. Since the market was mostly falling, the spot price would sink faster than forward prices. Try as I might to work around this spread, we started losing two to three cents a pound each time we rolled over our long positions.

These losses started piling up and came to the attention of François Décotterd, the General Manager. François was a good friend of Thibaud's father and also had a soft spot for me, because he was married to a woman from Moncton who'd come to Switzerland as an au pair. Whenever we met at the coffee machine, François would strike up a conversation about the Gaspé Peninsula, where he loved to go boating and skidooing and which I knew from hitchhiking. One day last January while Thibaud was away skiing, François asked me to step into his office.

"What's this margin call we got from your broker?"

I read the telex from Myers and Sidley. They wanted forty thousand dollars within three days, warning that if we failed to comply, they were entitled to unwind enough of our positions to settle the balance in their favour.

"Roasters are buying farther and farther forward to take advantage of the drop in coffee prices and the dollar," I explained.

"So?"

"We can't cover with physical coffee because shippers are getting nervous. They won't sell to us that far out. We have to buy contracts instead and we get screwed when they run out."

"Surely Thibaud can see that."

"He thinks we're covered on paper…"

The upshot is that François assigned me to investigate the cost prices of lots we'd sold in the past six months. It was a mammoth task requiring me to sift through shipping documents, warehouse data and bank statements. Thibaud found me buried in this paperwork when he came back from vacation and didn't like what he saw.

"Have you ever noticed how much weight our coffee loses in Italy?" I asked him, holding up a copy of a warehouse receipt. "A lot more than in Switzerland. Are they stuffing their aprons, or what?" I'd long suspected the Italians of ripping us off but Thibaud loved doing business with the agency in Genoa. He called it *Comedia dell'arte* when they cried on the phone, begging him to lower his price. Which he often did.

"Remember the dollars we reserved to buy those three containers of Haiti last March?" I continued, waving a forex statement. "The coffee only cost fifty-two thousand finally instead of fifty-nine. We had to sell seven thousand dollars back to bank twelve centimes lower, between the fall in the currency and the bank's spread." Thibaud's features contorted into outrage. He stood up without a word and marched down the hall to François's office. He hadn't come back by the time I knocked off work that evening.

Our relationship changed completely from then on. We rarely spoke. He watched me sulkily as I went on calculating the cost prices, nattering under his breath that they didn't mean anything since he'd paired the sales with other purchases. He also muttered "Coffee or not coffee" a number of times to himself before I realized he was alluding to *Hamlet*. It hadn't occurred to me that his job meant so much to him: it was his whole life. By weaving together strands of gossip I'd heard in the three years we'd worked face to face, I reconstructed how his career had started and evolved. Basically, he'd never grown up. His father had pleaded with François to find him a sandbox to play in at the import firm, having concluded that though intuitive he wasn't cut out for university and preferred model trains to girls. That was how he'd landed in the coffee trade, which he adopted as immediately as I had. François groomed him for a while before being swamped by more important matters. Content to collect the federal subsidies that the firm could claim for keeping mandatory stockpiles of green coffee, among other imports, he gave Thibaud free rein and was surprised to see the volumes grow, unaware that with no supervision, his friend's quirky son had become a pushover salesman with delusions of genius and little notion of the devil in detail. Meanwhile. the firm was expanding but had no IT resources yet, making it difficult to keep track of how much profit each of the departments – canned goods, mushrooms, spices, sugar, coffee and other commodities – was generating. François was no fool, though, and with coffee prices sliding since early 1986 in tandem with the US dollar, by the time of the first margin call he already suspected that Thibaud's sandbox had sprung a leak. In the meantime, I was digging my own grave with the cost-price calculations.

"The coffee department has to be downsized," François informed me soberly. He paused and then brightened. "I've already put out some feelers. Arlaud is looking for a second-in-command with your profile. You'd be in the big times there, with a better salary. I'll be glad to recommend you."

"That would be very kind," I answered without thinking. "Thank you."

Actually, I had mixed feelings as my love affair with coffee had soured. Rather than stripping a beauty naked, I wondered if I hadn't wandered into a blind alley. "There's no future in it that I can see," was the verdict of a trader in Zurich who called to chat occasionally. He was quitting the sector to become a buyer for Lindt. When I blabbed to him about our trading strategy, he scoffed: "That doesn't work. The only way to make money these days is to sell short and cover at the last minute. If the owners will let you."

I thought of going back on unemployment and looking for something new, like him. But in the end, with a wife and two kids to feed, a bird in hand – even a lame duck like coffee – was at least something to put on the table. Arlaud's size would be an advantage if the coffee trade became a war of attrition, I reasoned. The transparency of the back-to-back deals we did in the Non-Member segment even reassured me for a while. Until the market crashed and business dried up. The spot price in New York didn't stop at a dollar a pound. I watched tight-lipped with my fellow traders and their assistants as it continued its inexorable decline through ninety cents and then eighty. Time, the great illusion, seemed to slow and then stop altogether. But it wasn't time that froze, it was we who froze in time. We could have been ancient mariners stuck in the doldrums, our sails limp as a soggy biscuit, praying for a breath of wind, asking ourselves how long it would be until the shipworms ate through the hull of our stricken vessel.

"First capitulation, then resignation," was how Dario, my colleague at the Robusta Desk, sums up the mood when I meet him in the parking lot this morning. He opens the trunk of his car and asks me to lend a hand, indicating one of the strap handles of a bulging Ikea bag.

"What's all this stuff?"

"I'm gonna take my lawn-mower engine apart and replace the gaskets."

"I can see you're as busy as we are."

Dario and I clock in and ride the elevator to the third floor with the Ikea bag between us. The problem for him, he explains, isn't so much the fall in prices. He only trades futures now and his aim is to straddle each day's highs and lows, finishing when London closes with no residual risk. The market can go whichever way it wants: what he needs is daily amplitude and this has narrowed dismally. Each day amounts to a long waiting game, like trolling for perch, he's saying when we arrive in the aisle alongside our offices. We find the way blocked by two security guards standing with folded arms on either side of the trolley they've parked at the door to the Arabica Desk. Inside, Alex is bent over his desk, sorting through the contents of an open drawer.

"Looks like somebody got the sack. I'll manage from here," Dario murmurs, clasping both handles of his bag and pushing past the guards with a curt nod.

I take my seat and start reading the telexes that arrived overnight. From time to time I look up to watch Alex through the glass partition as he clears out his desk, coolly examining each item before handing it to the security guard by the door. The guard spends equal time examining the item before passing it on to his colleague, who deposits it in the cardboard box on the trolley. A dispute erupts when the security man refuses to let Alex remove his diary. I can hear muffled shouts as Alex, his face livid, continues to protest until he finally grabs his phone and then paces the floor, fuming, while waiting for someone to answer. When they do, he wrangles a while longer before giving up and slamming the receiver down with a thud that penetrates the partition. In all, the desk-clearing exercise lasts almost an hour, during which the remaining traders and assistants stroll in nonchalantly, stop in their tracks and stand agape, watching what's happening. I nearly burst out laughing at one point, they remind me so much of the fish in Monty Python's *The Meaning of Life* exchanging phlegmatic "Good mornings" as they swim back and forth in the aquarium. Until one suddenly exclaims: "Hey, look! Howard's being eaten!"

"Arschloch" is all Christoph has to say when he comes in at nine, casting a contemptuous glance at the now empty chair next to Luc. He heard the story from Lorenzo yesterday after I left.

"Why did they give him the axe?"

"For exceeding his limit."

"What a jerk! How far was he in the hole?"

"Three hundred thousand or so." Christoph is disgusted. "We can kiss our bonuses goodbye this year."

I'm avid for more details but he has no time to waste this morning. For the first time in weeks, he's busy, preparing to go to Algiers tomorrow in hopes of signing with the contracting agency. There's little left to do, really. Together we've read the tender specification five times; the dispute resolution clause provides for arbitration in London. The agent in Paris has already negotiated on our behalf and the offer we gave him will remain firm for another forty-eight hours, notwithstanding an unlikely rally in the Robusta market. The three shippers we selected based on previous business and samples I inspected have formed a consortium. The largest is ready to load fifteen hundred of the twenty-five hundred tonnes the Algerians want on a single vessel under a charter-party with Great Eastern. If the contracting agency gives us the nod while Christoph is in Algiers, he'll call me from his hotel and I'll confirm the purchase with the head of our consortium in Singapore.

Nobody has explained Alex's dismissal to me in detail when I leave for the Parc des Bastions at lunchtime. I'm actually wondering what the idiot might be doing at the moment after his ignominious exit this morning – getting drunk? lying low with video tapes? hastily preparing a solo beach holiday? – when lo and behold, there he is watching a chess game with folded arms at the park entrance. I'm hoping he won't see me but he does and hails me.

"I've got something for you," he says without a hello, fishing a booklet out of his bag and pressing it into my free hand. I read the title: *100 Chess Openings for White and Black*. He doesn't wait for a thank you. "It's your level. I'm on to something more advanced." A pause. "You probably think I'm a jerk."

"Not at all."

"That's what I like about you, Ben," he lies in turn. "You're no back-biter."

"So, what are you gonna do now, play chess professionally?"

"Bernauer have already approached me."

"*What*? They want a guy who half-sank his last employer?"

"I'm into Elliott waves. They know that's where the action is."

I roll my eyes. "Sounds like a new plague remedy calling for dragon's blood."

"Dunno what you're talking about. But I laid it all out to Bernauer's coffee boss and they know I won't make the same mistake twice."

"What about your non-compete clause?"

"Those things don't hold up in court." He waves to a short man wearing designer sunglasses who has just come through the gate. "Salut Gérard! On joue une partie?" Our conversation is over.

Thomas is sitting on our appointed bench, ogling the trim figures of two young tourists a few feet away in front of the Reformation Wall. I tell him about my encounter with Alex. "What were you expecting, remorse?" he asks in the offhand manner he adopts when absorbed in something more interesting.

"What I can't figure out is why nobody spotted it immediately. The whole point of Icarus is to make sure we don't hide any funny business."

"From what I heard," Thomas stubs out his cigarette, still observing the two women who are now consulting a Michelin Guide, "It started with wash trading."

"Selling to himself, to pump up volume."

"The boys upstairs liked it, made the company look good. But Swagger Stick (Thomas has a nickname for everyone, mine is Gentle Ben) got it into his cocky head that the coffee agreement was going to be saved. He marked his wash sales as short futures that he never actually bought."

"But they must've seen that the physical quantities and contract quantities didn't match."

"Except that Icarus caps the number of open shorts. The guy who monitors your department's positions thought they were invisible."

So that was it: the line about wave theory was bullshit; he had misread the fundamentals.

"Did you know what was going on?"

"I knew he was in trouble. I can't fly any better than Icarus but I keep my ear to the ground."

"And you didn't say anything?"

"He was gonna get canned sooner or later."

"Christoph is sick of seeing the rest of the department lose money. Why don't they just quit?"

Thomas's gaze follows the two young women as they move on. "The Arlauds have deep pockets. They're betting that other outfits will throw in the towel first."

"Well, I'm getting sick of the shambles we're in. Without the agreement prices have gone through the floor. The Algerians are the only ones in the market. Everyone else is spooked."

"They'll be back." Thomas unwraps his sandwich, takes a bite and chews thoughtfully. "People with a wider perspective say your agreement wasn't working. It was a nice idea but flawed from the start. Prices would be higher today if it hadn't existed."

"Whaddya mean? The agreement was meant to stabilize prices with export quotas. So growers would get a fair shake and pay their workers a decent wage." (Pity Ademir isn't here, he would be crying 'Hear, hear!') "And consumers could easily afford a few extra cents a pound, in the rich countries anyway."

"Seems it suited a lot of people. Farmers made enough money to stay in business even if they were inefficient and should've been looking for alternatives. Their governments were happy too. They used the export revenues to buy arms and hold onto power when they should've been booted out long ago." He takes another bite of his sandwich and chews. "Sound familiar?"

At first I don't see the parallel, as usual. But then, as clear as the sunlight illuminating the stern face of Jean Calvin opposite us, it hits me. The news from Eastern Europe has been grabbing headlines for the past two months. Thomas was right about Hungary being next after Poland: they opened their border with

Austria, allowing thousands of East Germans to flee to the West. Last week, a huge crowd jeered Erich Honecker and went on a rampage during East Germany's fortieth-birthday celebration. The pro-democracy movement is spreading like wildfire.

"You mean communism, a nice idea but flawed."

He nods. "It's bankrupt. Defeated, like fascism."

I observe the four Reformers clutching their bibles, devout champions of another cause that swept northern Europe and locked horns with the Habsburgs in one of the Continent's longest and most brutal conflicts ever.

"At least we won without a third world war."

Thomas can see I'm eyeing the monument. "Take a good look. History could soon be a museum. It won't have any more actors, only caretakers."

"Who says so?"

"An American philosopher, Francis Fukuyama. He thinks that with the end of the Cold War we've come to the end of history. Liberalism is the only ideology left standing."

The words 'Cold War' send a shiver down my spine. Why, I can't say. The last time I thought consciously about the standoff between America and the USSR was during the anti-Pershing II missile demonstrations in Germany. Maybe they reminded me of an article I'd read about the anti-Bomarc protests in Canada twenty-five years ago. I was just a kid then, living up north in Churchill. There was a military base nearby. I remember seeing US tanker planes through the perimeter fence of the airport. They had bright orange bands near their tail sections. Dad told me before he died two years ago that the base was demolished in 1981.

I'm alone the next day at work. Our buyer in Bahrain wants a container of Costa Rica and a container of cardamom. This is his first inquiry in five months. He reminds me that he sells the coffee unroasted from the back of his shops and insists that it be very green. Funny how Arabs are fixated on that colour. Christoph told me that once an importer found our beans too pale and had them soaked in green dye. At lunchtime Cerny, the boss of Kospol, calls from Prague for an offer. When I ask what the mood is in Czechoslovakia, he pretends not to understand. They've ordered him not to talk politics, no doubt. I spend most of the afternoon reading the paper. An editorial on Fukuyama's essay catches my eye. The columnist notes that while liberal democracy has triumphed, so has consumerism. Should we cheer? At five o'clock I phone our shipper in San José to check his price and then revert to the buyer in Bahrain. He's disappointed that his grade of Costa Rica hasn't come down much in price. I explain that the differentials of washed, high-grown varieties have shot up since the collapse of the agreement. He says he doesn't understand my English so I tell him quality coffee growers haven't dropped their pants like the Brazilians and if he wants really green beans, he has to pay top dollar. After more grumbling, he accepts.

At six thirty I'm back in the office with my second sandwich of the day. Christoph is supposed to call me from Algiers at seven and does so.

"We got the business." His tone is a mix of elation and relief.

"Allah be praised!" I exclaim before remembering that the phone at his hotel is probably tapped. "How's the weather?"

"Still the same." This is coded language informing me that the contracting agency agreed to our price. There will be no need to haggle with Darren Koh, our shippers' agent in Singapore, though I'll still have to confirm the purchase tonight by phone. After a few more words with Christoph, who regrets that I don't speak Swiss German (it would be so much easier to foil eavesdroppers), I hang up and dial Darren's number. No answer. I wait another half-hour and try again. Damn, still no answer! It's two a.m. in Singapore. He said he could be reached any time of the day or night and gave me his home phone number as well, just in case. Do I dare call him there?

By nine p.m. I've tried his office three more times. At nine fifteen my phone rings and I jump on it. It's my wife. She wants to know what I'm up to. Things have been strained between us lately. I try to explain calmly but she senses my mounting irritation.

"How do I know you're not with your secretary?"

I blow up. "What the hell would I be doing in this glass cage with our secretary? It's the last place I'd take her!"

The exchange heats up some more, then we both break off. I slam down the receiver and dial Darren's home number. I let it ring eight times and am about to give up when a woman answers with a groggy voice. I apologize profusely. She cuts me off, saying none too worried that Darren hasn't come home yet. I explain I have to confirm a deal with him worth three million dollars. She's alert in a jiffy and obsequious to boot, promising to call all the bars he haunts and get back to me if she can't find him.

With nothing to do but wait and hope, I take a telex from my In-tray. It's Benson's report to Jarvis in New York on the day's cocoa developments. I rarely bother with these missives, which brim with political trivia about Ivory Coast, Nigeria, Ghana and Togo and moan how tough it's getting to squeeze out any kind of profit. Futures prices in London are slumping towards a thousand pounds a tonne. Today, Benson bought twenty-five tonnes of Mozambique because it looked too cheap to pass up. His litany trails off into a whimper: "This market is a bitch…" And the wily bitch is screwing us all, I'd like to add.

At ten fifteen Darren calls. His wife tracked him down at the Yard Pub on River Valley Road. "She keeps me on a long leash," he jokes, slurring the sibilants.

"You lucky bugger."

His laugh ends in a fit of coughing. "Scuse me, whisky and cigars…" They started drinking at midnight and he completely forgot the time. Of course, his offer is still valid. Yes, we have a firm deal for two thousand five hundred tonnes of EK-1, C+F Oran, November shipment. He'll ring the shippers and Great Eastern first thing in the morning with the good news. "You gonna take your secretary out to celebrate?"

"I'm going home to bed."

"You Swiss are so damn serious. I'm having one more for the road!"

The next three weeks go by more quickly. A gentle breeze has come up and our sails are straightening. We're moving again. Thomas was right, as he is so often: our customers can't wait forever for the market to bottom out and are straggling back, albeit with limited orders. Christoph has perked up too since returning from Algeria. After slacking off for two and a half months, arriving late in the morning and taking extended lunch breaks four times a week to play tennis, he has recovered some of his hard-nosed determination. "What can go wrong now?" he asks with calm reassurance when the telex arrives announcing that the *Artemonas*, carrying the largest load of EK-1 – one thousand five hundred tonnes – has sailed from Lampung for Oran.

Three days later, on November the ninth, I rush back to the office after lunch bursting with excitement. I'm eager to share the news I heard at the cafeteria: the spokesman for East Berlin's Communist Party this morning announced that East German citizens will be able to cross the border freely to the West from midnight tonight: the Wall is coming down!

I stop in mid-stride. Christoph is hunched over the desktop, his face in his hands. When I ask, frightened, what's wrong, without looking up he shoves a telex towards me with his elbow. Picking it up, I recognize Great Eastern's call sign. The company informs us that the *Artemonas* has unexpectedly put into Port Blair in the Andaman Islands. Port firefighters are battling a blaze that broke out in the crew's cabins. The captain has absconded.

Christoph's voice croaks under the hands covering his face. "What does 'absconded' mean, Ben?"

Mom

Geneva, December 1989

I think I know who Danny's father is, or could easily be. The circumstantial evidence is in any case compelling, though of course the really stunning thing is that it has come to light here in Geneva. And now, far into the future. The discovery began with the slides that Mom brought on a visit just over a year ago. The house in Winnipeg had become too much for her since Dad passed away, and she was starting to sort out the basement in view of moving to a downtown apartment. Neither Dave, now an oil engineer in Fort McMurray, nor Beth, an English teacher in Nanaimo, wanted anything bulky. Nor did I, I insisted when Mom asked yet again if I had plans to return to Canada. But yes, a small keepsake or two would be nice. As a consequence, when she arrived in October last year, besides clothes and books in English for the children her second suitcase contained a pair of ookpiks and the slides in two blue and white plastic trays. Finding them had been a surprise, Mom told me on our way into town from the airport. In her mind they'd been lost, like our baby pictures and the family's other modest heirlooms, in the trunk that went missing when we moved to BC. But stashed in a corner of the basement, unopened for over twenty years, sat a box marked *Churchill*. And buried under the memorabilia inside – embroidered mukluks, a wolverine skin, a painting of ptarmigan on rocks, stone carvings wrapped in tissue paper and a hymn book illustrated with photos of missionaries and natives – a dozen trays of slides lay snugly arranged on the bottom. Mom viewed them, made a selection and composed two trays each for Dave, Beth and me as souvenirs.

"Do you remember?" She asked, peering out the window of the bus at the buildings lining Rue de la Servette. How narrow the thoroughfare must seem to her, I thought, compared with Portage Avenue in Winnipeg! "Dad developed the films with a young Mountie in the bathroom of the RCMP barracks."

I observed her closely. This was her first visit since the funeral and it hadn't struck me then but she was ageing. It wasn't her hair. She had earned her grey hair and would never dye it,; a fact she liked to repeat. What I noticed was that she looked a bit frail, while still remarkably pretty, and had shrunk. She'd always been short, a bare five feet, and had now managed to lose a valuable inch. Could this be the same Mom I watched plucking geese in my earliest memory of her, probably at the age of four? That would have been in the kitchen of our tiny house in Norton. She was yanking out wing feathers with what was surely amazing strength for a woman her size, tensing muscles formed by years of butter churning and other chores on the farm. I'd gazed, fascinated, as she lit a candle and slowly rotated the geese over the flame to burn off the stubble. My memory was rife with the pungent smell of singing, blood and flesh and with a vivid image of the birds' pale, bumpy skin blotched purple where Dad had shot them, their down and feathers heaped on sheets of newspaper. How could I recall all that and not the darkroom where Dad developed his films in Churchill?

"I remember he used to swear when he forgot to remove the lens cap before taking a picture."

With a viewer borrowed from a neighbour, Mom and I looked through the slides when we were alone a few evenings later. She had an extraordinary recall of names and events that to me meant little or nothing. Many pictures were of ships and the harbour, including scenes from a ride on a black and red tugboat.

"Don't you remember?" Mom asked. "We went out with the pilot to meet a ship in the bay."

"Doesn't ring a bell." I squinted at the picture of Beth and me huddled in a tarp. Beth had a forearm raised to shield her face from the spray. My head was bowed.

"You were miserable."

"If you say so." I tried to read my expression but the features were too small and fuzzy.

"Dad's camera didn't have a zoom," Mom explained. "It was fine for landscapes but not for close-ups."

"Was that when we went down the line on a gas car and almost collided with a train on the way back?" I wondered, inspecting another picture. It showed Dave and me posing with what looked like jackfish near a bridge over a small river. The gas car episode wasn't so much a memory as a story that I'd heard Dad tell a number of times. Mom told it to me again. We'd gone fishing southwest of town and were surprised a couple of miles from home by the light of an unscheduled freight train far ahead. It wasn't clear whether the train was manoeuvring in the railyard or heading slowly towards us. To play it safe, we pulled the gas car off the track (no small feat) and waited. But the light now seemed motionless and, as it was getting dark, we hauled the gas car back up onto the track and set off again. We were reaching a good clip when it suddenly became obvious that the light ahead was looming larger. There wasn't time to take the gas car off the track! Dad ordered Dave and me to jump off while he raced for the switch three hundred yards ahead. He made it in the nick of time!

"He could've been killed," Mom concluded with a heavy sigh. I recalled Dad using those same words in the first person.

"Who's that?" I asked when we came to the only other picture of me. It was summer and I was sitting on a flat rock with a boy my age. We were both wearing green Scout shirts, jeans and running shoes. He had more achievement badges on his arm than I did. His hair was longish and black, his tan darker than mine. I was smiling at the camera while he was looking away. He reminded me of Neil Young on the cover of the Crosby, Stills, Nash and Young album.

"That's Danny. He was your closest friend. You must remember him, surely."

I didn't. I struggled to scrutinize his face but again the features were too small and fuzzy. We were dwarfed by the background, a chaotic jumble of boulders stretching far behind us. It could have been the scaly back of a gigantic, primordial serpent basking in the wan sun before returning to the bay, visible as a strip of blue beyond.

"The first day he came to call, he told me he was going to protect you."

There was a rustle, like a movement behind a curtain that opened a crack, and for an infinitesimal space of time I saw Mom clearly. Much younger, and not there in my living room. We were standing on the top of rickety steps in front of a porch. She was talking to me with an amused smile. There was someone else at the bottom of the steps but I couldn't see who. The crack closed and the curtain hung limp.

I didn't look at the slides again or even think of them until this summer, during a lunchtime conversation with Thomas in the park. We somehow latched onto his reputation for getting into arguments in the mailroom. I mentioned hearing from Barbie that he'd received a reprimand.

"She should stop spreading vicious rumours and spread her legs more," he snorted, before admitting he'd been warned more than once. "It's true, I'm a troublemaker," he confessed. "I started young." He told me how he'd been expelled from his Gymnasium in Thun for leading a mutiny against the school's gym teacher. "We piled him into a locker and left him there overnight." The recollection brought a fiendish grin to his face. "I was a hero for a day. Everybody hated the bastard."

"So, if you got kicked out of school, where did you do all your reading? As a night watchman?" It was a serious question. He'd never talked about his past and had the withdrawn look of someone who'd spent long hours alone.

"Of sorts," he answered. "I worked in the merchant navy. Ten years as a deck hand and thirty more as a stores officer in Arlaud's fleet. When I finally had enough of boiled potatoes and the smell of diesel oil under my fingernails, even after a shower, I applied for a transfer to dry land here in Geneva." His voice turned bitter. "I'd had a few run-ins with captains in my day, so the only thing they would offer me was this shit job delivering mail." He wiped the sweat from beneath the shock of grey hair on his brow.

"Forty years at sea!" I marvelled. I'd read about Arlaud's merchant fleet in the company brochure. Now a separate entity, it was developed with federal subsidies to ensure Switzerland's food supply during the Second World War and later to bolster commercial independence. The ships were named after Uri, Ticino, Valais and other Swiss cantons. "You could've read *War and Peace* ten times over."

"What I didn't spend wisely on women and booze I wasted on books. Reading kept me from getting into fights with my shipmates. Now it keeps me from wringing their necks in the mailroom."

I felt sorry for him. His temper had dogged him throughout his life. "But you didn't just read books all those years. You must've seen a lot of the world."

His eyes lit up. "You bet your ass I did! Up to the end of the fifties they kept me on the North and South Atlantic runs, hauling grain and soybeans to Rotterdam. But from then on, I plied the Mediterranean, Africa, India, the Far East, you name it."

"Did you go to Canada?"

"We called at Halifax and Montreal after the war. I bummed around those places while we were laying over."

"What about Churchill?"

His eyes narrowed. "Port Churchill? Yeah, I'm pretty sure we went there too …"

"It's Churchill, not Port Churchill," I corrected him but he wasn't listening.

"I could check my logbook. Why?"

"I lived there a long time ago."

"Way up on the edge of nowhere?"

"Yep. But I don't remember much. It's as if my mind blocked most of it out." I told him about not recognizing my best friend.

"If it's any consolation, I've forgotten half the ignoramuses I sailed with."

The subject changed to politics and no more was said about Churchill. Until last Monday, the day after Mom arrived again, this time to spend Christmas with us. Thomas and I were still meeting in the park. We both enjoyed being outdoors, despite the cold. It was lunchtime and a skiff of snow blanketed the ground as I strolled through the gate. The chess pieces lay scattered around the board like a discomfited army. Berezina—the name echoed in my head. Market commentators have been using it as a trope for defeat, comparing the rout in coffee to Napoleon's calamitous retreat from Russia.

"The French actually won that battle," Thomas pointed out, opening his beer can with a practised hand, "Although they suffered heavy losses."

I told him my mother was here and I'd be on holiday next week. He suddenly remembered having consulted the logbook of his sea voyages. He'd been to Churchill three times in alternating years: 1947, 1949 and 1951. His only recollection was of the last call.

"That's when I had septicaemia." He took a long swig of beer. "I was already sick leaving Europe. Should've gone to a dentist in Holland before the infection in my gums got into my bloodstream. By the time we made it to Port Churchill, I was so weak they had to carry me on a stretcher. There were guys in uniform. Does that sound right?"

I thought a second. "That would've been at the military hospital in Fort Churchill. How long did you stay?"

"I saw in my logbook that I arrived on the *Neuchâtel* in late August and left six weeks later on a different ship. That's how I remember being sick there."

"Did you visit the town?"

"They must've let me out of hospital at some point. I know I spent a while at a hotel near the port. And I know I saw the film *All About Eve* at a cinema there."

There was a ripple, then a flash. "It wasn't the Igloo Theatre, by any chance?"

His startled look told me his memory had been jogged like

mine. "Christ, I think it was! A rowdy place, full of drunks. I'd already run into a couple of them at the beer parlour and we'd reached an understanding, if you see what I mean. They started tormenting a young woman when the show ended. She was alone and it was getting nasty, so I told them to lay off. I took her by the arm and steered her out the door."

"You mean you stood up for a harassment victim?"

"I'm kinder than you give me credit for."

"Was she pretty?"

"Well, you've gotta like her kind but…" I saw from his knit eyebrows that an image had formed in his mind. "…Yeah, she was quite the looker. Beautiful eyes."

"Her kind… Indian?"

"Half, she said."

"So, you got to know her?"

"Oh, I got to know her all right. She took me in till my ship came. And you know what?"

"What?"

"She spoke French. Good French, I remember, not that joual you hear in Quebec."

I was about to point out that Québécois French had come a long way since he hung out with dockers in East-end Montreal, when I had an idea.

"Why don't you come for supper this week and look at those slides of Churchill? My mom is about your age. You two could reminisce about the fifties, when I was still running around in diapers."

To my astonishment, Thomas accepted after little hesitation. I'd piqued his interest, though how wasn't clear. They say that people his age turn nostalgic, so maybe he was curious for a glimpse of the town where he'd been stranded nearly forty years ago. I couldn't imagine his conquest at the Igloo Theatre meaning much to him – not among the countless wenches he must have met from Rio to Rangoon. But who was I to judge?

"I'll scrounge up a slide projector and a screen," he offered.

It was all arranged in the next couple of days and the dinner-cum-slide-show took place this evening. After introducing Thomas to my wife, the kids and Mom, I left them to get acquainted and busied myself in the kitchen preparing the meal. Peals of laughter, including from the children, reassured me that Thomas was keeping them all well entertained. He wasn't a social misfit by any stretch, just a man whose solitary path had placed him at several removes from shallowness and predictability. After bringing out the vegetables and calling everyone to the dining-room table, I returned a few minutes later with the pièce de résistance: a platter of orange duck.

"Ben was born on the first day of duck season," Mom beamed as we passed around the bowls and held the platter for each other. "His dad was still a game warden then and he had to check hunters that day after driving me to the hospital. In the next town, six miles away. The road hadn't been paved yet. It was full of potholes, I remember."

"So that's why Ben's brains are scrambled!" Thomas cut in, making everyone laugh and making me turn red, which drew more laughter from the children.

After dinner, while my wife and I put the kids to bed, Mom and Thomas retired to the living room. When I joined them half an hour later, I could see from Mom's cosy posture and flushed appearance that Thomas had been talking her up, the lecherous son of a bitch.

"Show time!" I broke in, which didn't stop Mom from continuing to prattle while Thomas and I mounted the projector and screen. She was eager to see Thomas' reaction to the numerous views of ships and the harbour. She wasn't disappointed, for he knew ships like other guys knew football players and immediately recognized the first vessel by the name on her bow.

"The *Zinnia*!" He exclaimed. "She was built in Japan in the early fifties and flew the Cypriot flag, if I'm not mistaken. Here she's middle-aged." General cargo ships have a lifespan of twenty-five years or so, he explained, more than double that of the dry bulk carriers he'd sailed on in his early days. We saw half a dozen of these in subsequent pictures, though none belonged to Arlaud's fleet. One ship stood out from the pack with her gleaming white bridge and cranes: the *Warkworth*, freshly built and registered in Britain. Dad had been invited for a drink on board with the captain, Mom remembered.

She had many fond memories of Churchill, she told us. She'd enjoyed an active social life there, thanks to her involvement with the church and to Dad's position as Indian agent, Legion member and Justice of the Peace. Her anecdotes ran seamlessly together concerning the views around town. The projector and screen revealed details that had escaped us on the viewer. One was the rear end of a polar bear, visible as a tiny, yellowish-white blob far down our street. An excited discussion ensued about the bear that had brushed past our house as it skirted Mr. Panchenko's ladder propped up against the federal building next door. The story had since evolved into various versions. Mine – I don't know where it came from – held that Mom was baking pies in the kitchen and turned around to set one down on the window sill when she found herself face to face with the snarling bear. To titillate audiences, especially in Europe, I've sometimes added that the animal didn't eat her pie but would have gladly eaten her if it had been able to! Mom corrected me: she wasn't making pies, she was ironing on the table. And she got very mad at Beth for running after that mean, hungry-looking bear with friends picked up along the way. She also recalled a hilarious send-up in which a neighbour imitated Mr. Panchenko playing toreador with the bear after being knocked off his ladder and spilling the red paint on a rag, which he used as a cape to taunt the beast.

Thomas laughed heartily at all this. He hadn't mentioned being sick in Churchill so I presumed he had his reasons and didn't bring it up. Nor did I weigh in during Mom's accounts of the tugboat ride and gas car adventure. Although she often made me a significant character in her narrative, I didn't feel part of it. It was all so remote. I preferred the pictures that didn't concern me and imagined them concealing stories of my own invention. These ranged in believability from commonplace to romantic to supernatural. I imagined the dogsled parked in front of Tthe Bay belonging to a trapper who was inside selling his furs. He'd already seen eighty winters, as the Cree would say, and was weighing the advantages of moving into town. He flipped a silver dollar on the counter to decide whether to do so. Two hundred years earlier, the embrasure in the high stone wall of Prince of Wales Fort served as a perch for an Orkney lad indentured to the Hudson's Bay Company. Unknown to him then, he was in limbo between the bleak homeland he'd turned his back on and the new trading post upriver where he would be promoted to factor, take a country wife and never look back again. The wreck of the *Ithaka*, twelve miles east of Churchill, stood high and dry at low tide where she'd run aground in a storm in 1960. Passers-by had sighted ghostly figures weaving on her deck, bathed by the northern lights. Some said they were the flickering souls of Jens

Munk's dead shipmates, who had wandered the coast for three hundred and forty years and now gathered on the abandoned hulk in a forlorn hope that it would take them home at last.

"Do you remember your Scout leader, Father Gilles?"

Mom's voice startled me out of my reverie. They were talking about the picture of Danny and me that now filled the screen.

"No, I don't," I managed a timely reply, bringing my jarred attention to bear on the slide. The image of myself, skinny and cross-eyed at the age of twelve, was an embarrassment. It was one of those unbecoming fossils that ought to stay buried in their recess, far back in the passage of time. I was more sympathetic in my observation of Danny, though what struck me, like the first time I'd viewed this picture, was the direction of his gaze—away from the camera and over the muddle of rocks towards the bay. Did his attitude also conceal a story?

"Father Gilles became bishop of the region after we left," Mom continued. "The Catholics had a large mission in Churchill."

While Thomas recalled how he'd tried Scouts but felt silly saluting, and sillier still reciting the pledge, I stretched forward in my chair to get a closer look at Danny's face. To no avail: it blurred even more, becoming a formless mass of brownish light and shadow. Perhaps because of its very elusiveness I longed to touch it. But in the instant my hand started to quiver, the image was swept away. Thomas, who was waving the remote control while joking to the others about saluting in the merchant navy, had inadvertently pressed the forward button.

"Your colleague is a real card," Mom remarked after he left. She and I were alone in the kitchen, cleaning up.

I told her he'd been kicked out of high school and got into

fights at work."

"That's strange," she shook her head. "He doesn't come across as someone who flies off the handle."

"He can be civilized when he puts his mind to it. Even kind, he says." My own mind was still haunted by the image of Danny. I asked Mom if he and I got into trouble together.

She set down the pan she was drying and thought for a moment. "Well, I remember Dad having a fit when he found the two of you lighting candles under the house. In the crawl space. He was afraid the old newspapers would catch fire and burn the place down."

It was my turn to shake my head. "We did some dumb things as kids."

"Well, Danny got into worse trouble on his own. He used to haunt the railroad yard at night, when you were in bed. Once, the watchman caught him. His mother told me what he got up to there but I've forgotten. She was raising him alone and couldn't manage."

I unfolded Mom's hideaway bed in the living room while she made us a pot of tea. She was still thinking about Danny's mother when I joined her again. "I knew Rose-Marie very well," she recollected, pouring a cup for each of us. "She volunteered every year for our rummage sale at the Anglican Church. Even though she was a staunch Catholic. She was such a good person and so good at everything: mending, pressing, removing ground-in stains…"

"So, my partner in petty crime didn't have a father," I half-interrupted, hoping to steer her train of thought back to Danny.

"No, but Rose-Marie had man friends and people ostracized her for that. Especially that – what was her name? – Eileen, the RCMP sergeant's wife. She wouldn't talk to Rose-Marie or even look her in the face." She paused. "Though that's the way she acted with anyone who wasn't the right colour."

Danny's coppery complexion sprang into my mind. "You mean Danny's mother wasn't white?"

"She was Métis." Mom paused again and shot me a quizzical look. "Why are you staring?"

"Uh, sorry… I just remembered something about work." The truth is that for a split-second I'd been standing in a dark porch piled high with winter gear. A woman framed by light from the living room behind her was observing me with doe-like eyes while I explained something. Then she turned her head, called a name followed by some strange-sounding words and vanished. Was that Danny's mother? Could she help explain his elusive character? "Tell me about her."

Mom was happy to oblige. I listened with rapt attention while she reminisced, more with her teacup than with me. Between sips and silences, she pieced together the tale that Rose-Marie had confided to her a quarter-century ago across the table where they mended second-hand clothes together.

She was born in southwestern Saskatchewan to a Stoney mother and a Scots father. She had no memory of them. The topsoil of their homestead blew away in the early thirties, leaving them destitute. When her mother died (nobody knew of what, but malnutrition doubtless played a role), her father took her to the mission in what was probably Gravelbourg, I will determine in an internet search years from now. He left her in the care of the nuns, who schooled her till she was fourteen and then put her to work in the laundry. They treated her well enough but not as an equal, and she ended up eloping at eighteen with a man in his late twenties. He did repair work at the Collège and dreamed like her of getting away. He was a full-blooded Cree who had learned woodsmanship with his uncle. He and Rose-Marie ran off to northern Manitoba, where the government was handing out trapline concessions. He built a cabin and taught her to snare rabbits, tan hides and speak Cree.

"But her first language must have been French," I prompted, "Since she went to a Catholic school."

"Oh yes, she was proud of her French. She learned English later and spoke with an accent." Mom drained the teapot into her cup. "Sorry, there's none left for you."

I brushed her apology aside, anxious to hear more about this woman who had inexplicably left an impression on me. How did she end up alone with Danny?

"She was happy in the bush. They were self-sufficient, trapping animals and making the long trek in spring to sell the furs." She paused again. "It was the start of their third winter. She was expecting again after a couple of miscarriages and this time it seemed to be going well…" Mom's tone turned grave. "…Until the tragedy."

I squirmed on my chair. "Tragedy?"

"Her man – his name was Daniel – drowned with his dog team," Mom shuddered. "When he didn't come home, she followed his trail on snowshoes and saw the runners of the sled sticking up through the ice. After a day alone in the cabin, staring out the window, she did the only thing she could do: walk the ninety miles down the river to Churchill. It took her four days."

"So, the baby was Danny."

"No, she lost it on the way." Here Mom had to stop to wipe away tears. "For months she was tortured by the thought of it being devoured by wolves… But somehow, she found the fortitude to go on… To Churchill, I mean. She was a remarkable woman."

I could feel my own eyes moistening. And then – or now, rather – it bursts inside me. The tiny inkling ve been toying with mushrooms into a wild, full-blown realization. I slap a hand over my mouth to cover a gasp. Thankfully, Mom interprets it as a yawn and gets up to carry our cups to the sink. Still fighting breathlessness, I wait for her to come back for the teapot. I have to ask, even though it shames me: "Who was Danny's father, then?"

Mom doesn't answer until she has turned her back while emptying the tea egg into the garbage. "She didn't say… She was going with a guy at the Harbours Board when we lived in Churchill. But he was new. Before that she must have turned a few other heads. She had the softest brown eyes…" Mom is facing me now and frowning. "You're staring again. Are you sure you're okay?"

Dazed would be an apt description. "The distress of the coffee market is catching up with me," I mumble and wish her a feeble goodnight. I'm still twining the flayed strands of narrative while preparing for bed. The coincidence defies belief and yet it's obvious: the woman Thomas delivered from torment in the Igloo Theatre was Rose-Marie! It's simply a matter of numbers, to begin with. In a town as small as Churchill, a young Métis woman living alone would have been a real outlier. Then there was her French, which Thomas praised and had to be unusually good if she'd been raised by nuns. Her eyes, finally, left an indelible imprint on us all. It could only be her.

More confounding, however, is the upshot this match has made possible. I'm still adding up the years as I slip under the covers. Preposterous as this new hunch seems, the timeframe fits so neatly I can't help buying it. Mom says that Danny and I were the same age, so he could easily have been conceived in the summer of 1951, when Thomas was stuck in Churchill. He didn't say how long Rose-Marie put him up, but the mere fact that they were lovers in that period makes him a prime paternity candidate. What's more, that summer would have been critical for Rose-Marie if it was the first after her ordeal in the bush. In a rough town where she had no family and possibly no friends yet either, I can imagine her welcoming the solace of a dashing sailor who spoke her language. And though this is pure speculation, I see a glint of Thomas the maverick in Danny's diverted gaze and in Mom's memory of him as a prowler who ran afoul of authority.

I fall asleep boggled by the singularity of it all. Two hours ago, I was sitting between a picture of a childhood friend on the edge of nowhere and a colleague two oceans away who could well be his father. It smacks of Infinite Improbability Drive; that wacky invention in *Hitchhiker's Guide to the Galaxy*. To be at such a fanciful vantage point, I would almost have to be everywhere at once!

Still dreaming, I half-awaken sometime later. To silence, save for my wife's faint, steady breathing and the occasional muffled steps of our sleepless upstairs neighbour. I've had this dream before. I'm standing on a pebble beach by a mountain lake. The children are building a stone tower that's about to collapse. They're younger. I walk to the water and look down. Already at the edge, the lake appears inky and deep. There is movement, though: the ghostly blue mass far below is alive. I strain my eyes and eventually see it's made of eerie, undulating shapes. They're fish—a huge school of them, pitching, yawing and curving. A pair dart towards the surface, turn tail in mid-course and dive back down into the writhing blue mass. Now a larger one has detached from the rest and is surging towards me. It hangs motionless, smooth and silvery, just beneath the surface.

Its nearness is tantalizing. I want to reach out and grab it. But as I lean down, it too arches and scoots back down into the netherworld. I'm fully awake now. Our neighbour has switched on music. I know what the dream means. The fish are my memories.

What to do? Tell Mom? No. She might still be acquainted with people who lived in Churchill. I don't want her spreading the feathers of gossip, even though I'm sure a good part of it is true. Tell Thomas? Tell him what? That he had and may still have a bastard son in Churchill? For all he knows, he has a gaggle of illegitimate kids. Others do. Genetic studies will one day show that the tall dark stranger is no myth, and they aren't all sailors on laytime. Ideally, love affairs should have neither consequences nor witnesses. Ideally, the one between Thomas and Rose-Marie was as intense as it was brief. He never went back to Churchill and never saw her again, except unwittingly in the blurred face of Danny this evening.

Soon Thomas won't see me anymore either. I've signed on with the documentary credits department of a bank in Lausanne. Christoph is fuming. He'll still hold a grudge when we run into each other a year from now.

"You were a tourist from the start."

"You can believe what you want, but I really fell in love with the business. It just wasn't the place to be." Pause. "Did the Algerians ever pay up?"

"We're still wrangling with the insurer they forced us to work with, but in any case, the shippers won't see a penny till the claim is settled." He has a new worry eating up half his time, he'll add ruefully: three containers blocked in Kuwait following the Iraqi invasion.

Although coffee will be one of the commodities I deal with

in my next job, I won't have any more skin in the game. I'll keep tabs on the market from a safe distance, as on the career of a former lover, reading avidly when it makes the news, and for the blink of an eye I'll relive a wrenching fall in futures prices or the intoxicating aroma of freshly roasted Sidamo.

What I'll really miss, for a while anyway, is meeting Thomas in the Parc des Bastions. In the few months I've known him, his mentoring has given added resonance to the tumultuous events unfolding on our doorstep. But perhaps it's just as well. Now I know something of his personal life, he'll come across more as a man than an encyclopaedia. For starters, he's not always right. The regime in Romania, which he thought would hang on for months or even years, has toppled. As I drift back into sleep, the Ceausescus are being held in an agricultural centre and on Christmas Day will be shot after a mocking trial before a drumhead court-martial. The episode will live on as the most spectacular in communism's downfall. If anything, though, it should be remembered instead as an ancient saga retold for the umpteenth time. Of the oppressed rising up against their oppressors, or of a ruthless shoe passing to the other foot. Not, in any case, as a highlight in the end of history. With hindsight, that view will seem Euro and chrono-centric, not to mention bombastic, akin to the speculation on the end of the world during the Black Death. When I get down to writing this, many more years hence, liberal democracy will be on the run. A new Cold War will be afoot. Nationalisms will be burning brightly, stoked by strongmen clinging to morphed ideologies and warped religions. Why would they want to be curators of a dusty museum when they can be generals goading on their troops? 'Time marches on,' Dad used to say philosophically. But he was wrong: it is history that marches on. Time is the road, not the army.

Part III

Jeff

Churchill, August 1964

Danny is watching from a bench as Mom, Beth and I climb off the train. It's a relief to see him after the long journey back and three weeks on my grandparents' farm with little to do there. Dad stayed home to launch his sport-whaling venture. Dave, who is saving up for university next year, came back after one week to work at The Bay. What's more, he spent most of that week helping around the farm, so he and I managed only one foray into the woods with a single partridge to show for it. Danny snickers: he can do better hunting ptarmigan on the tundra with his slingshot.

We meet the next afternoon on the pebble beach behind my house. The air is bracing and a mite chilly after the midsummer heat of the Interlake country. At least there are few bugs, thanks to the breeze and lack of vegetation. They drove us crazy at Scout camp in the first week of July, swarming around us in the millions. Our only respite came at night, when we closed the door and windows of the bunkhouse tight and hunted down every last mosquito and blackfly inside with a vengeance.

"Remember how they were waiting for us in the morning?" I call to Danny, who has started off. "Clouds of them, bloodthirstier than ever!" He's leading the way over the rocks towards the east. I observe how he stops every so often, not only to wait for me to catch up but also to survey the terrain ahead and set a course for us. Basically, he's staying as high as possible on the flattest boulders while skipping over the gaps between them and skirting the pools of water and slimy spots in their hollows. He never wastes a step, improvising to deal with unforeseen obstacles as they arise. I'll recognize this same savvy blend of strategy and tactics a few years from now in the way veteran snooker players achieve long runs, by first surveying the configuration of reds and coloureds on the table and then pocketing them one by one, applying English or backspin to the cue ball to obtain the required shape.

"I like bugs better than jam and toothpaste smeared inside my backpack," Danny calls back over his shoulder.

It takes me a second to clue in as I'd forgotten the prank. It was Jeff's work, obviously. Robin didn't come with us to Camp Nanuq. He and his mother had left for London, Ontario the day after school ended and they wouldn't be back until the third week of August. Jeff knew exactly what his mischief would lead to: Father Gilles tried to draw out a confession or denunciation by sending us all to bed with no supper and this merely bred more ill feeling towards Danny, whom Father Gilles showers with compliments and achievement badges—more even than on the other altar boys in the troop. They suspect this special treatment is a reward for his mother's considerable volunteer work, which is rumoured to include sexual favours. The good padre flirts openly with single women and, some say, imposes the law of the first night on those who want to be married in his church.

"At least we'll be rid of Jeff and Robin at school next year," I offer. They will be moving to the main building to start grade seven, along with Roger who failed but can't be held back a second time. Why am I thinking about school, though? We have three full weeks of summer holidays left and I'm anxious to explore the rocks along the shoreline. I've felt drawn to them ever since that morning, almost a year ago, when Danny appeared out of nowhere and warned me against jumping over a pool. I can sense an invisible force emanating from the brownish-grey granite—an aura of great age. The rocks around Churchill are two billion years old. The Quebec side of the bay has bedrock nearly as old as Earth itself, I'll learn one day.

"See that one?" Danny is pointing to an oddly shaped upright slab jutting out over the basin beside the boulder he's standing on. "That's Dinosaur Rock."

I examine the mass of stone protruding from the lip of the basin and, sure enough, it resembles a thick animal cut-out. The back and torso narrow into a slender neck ending with a wedge-shaped projection that could easily be the head of an Ornithomimus bowing to drink. "Amazing!" I whistle. "Are there more weird formations like this?"

"Lots. There's a group of rounded ones just up over the ridge," he nods to our right. "They look like a family of turtles."

The diversity of the shapes grows more striking as I pay closer attention to each monolith we pass. Soon they all start to resemble the petrified remains of strange creatures, an eldritch host forged eons ago in fiery chaos, fused and twisted by a mighty hand. Years from now, when I read A.M. Klein's "Portrait of the Poet as Landscape", I will recall how I longed to name and praise these rocks, in the same way the nth Adam in the poem names and praises his 'world but scarcely uttered'. Does it matter that his inventory is green and fertile whereas the rocks are a drab palette of barren greys and browns? They are standing witnesses of Creation, inarticulate but not at all mute.

Danny has veered left and stopped well ahead of me. When

I catch up to him, he's sitting on a flat-topped boulder five feet high at the water's edge.

"This is Bloody Altar," he informs me solemnly, gazing out over the bay.

"Why do they call it that?"

"If the tide was out, you could see the red stain at the bottom. Where a whale smashed into it."

I look at him askance. "When did that happen?"

"Who knows?" he shrugs. "A long time ago."

Below, the waves beat against the stone at regular intervals, each lifting a shower of fine spray. "That doesn't make sense," I say. The blood would've washed away when it happened. If it really did…"

He rounds on me, returning my disbelieving stare with an obstinate glare of his own. ""It did happen!" his voice rises above the wind. "And I tell you, the blood's in the rock!"

What can I answer? I puff out my cheeks and expel a breath between pursed lips. "If you say so."

The days that follow take us farther up the shore. I grow nimbler, more daring and surer-footed. Danny scampers ahead all the faster, covering longer distances before stopping to wait. I know he's not showing off. That's not his style. His style, I've concluded, is a sort of elusiveness. Perhaps he's so used to being alone that even together with me he needs time to himself—time to watch the belugas frolicking among the whitecaps, to take target practice with his slingshot and to whet the edge of the bone-handled knife he carries in a leather sheath strapped to his belt.

One afternoon he leads the way up the ridge. When I join him at the top, panting from the climb, I find myself overlooking the town cemetery on the other side. A wire fence separates it from the first two rows of cabins forming the upper part of Camp 10. How flimsy and forlorn the tiny shacks seem, even in summer, with their blistered paint and makeshift tepees (stick tripods draped with tattered blankets) behind them. The cemetery is dominated by a large cross with a stone statue of Jesus hanging from it and more statues of grieving women at his feet. Thirty yards from us down the hill, three Chipewyan children are playing tag among the rows of crosses marking the graves. Danny grips his slingshot, fits a small stone into the pocket and lets fly. One of the kids grabs his backside, spins around and gapes at us. He yells something to the others and all three flee towards the cabins.

Danny smirks as they stumble over the graves, upsetting bouquets of flowers. "Injuns," he calls the Chipewyan. This struck me as amusing at first, coming from a Métis, until I noticed how the Cree and Métis all mistreat the Chipewyan kids at school. The boys bully the boys while the girls make fun of the girls' clothes and hair. Some whites can be just as mean-spirited, scorning the Chipewyan as outcasts or even savages—the lowest of the low. As a result, they roam the town and the Fort in packs to defend themselves against aggression from all sides. Jeff, who's hanging out with Lennie and his pals while Robin is away, loves to torment them by pushing them into puddles. After a recent game of scrub, he snuck up behind a group with his bat and whacked a couple on the butt, viciously, while they were absorbed watching a game of marbles. But his sadism knows no bounds, as I find out on the Saturday after school starts. That afternoon, Danny says he has had enough of guiding me over the rocks and wants me to come with him to the railyard.

"What can we do there?"

"I wanna check out the old buildings some more."

"For what?"

"You can still find things lying around—nails, screws, rubber hoses, pipefittings... Stuff that might come in handy around the house or for my sled."

I follow his lead, lured by that small-town craving for novelty. The railway station is deserted except for half a dozen Chipewyan children of various ages loitering about the platform. Danny scowls at them. He says they're waiting for tourists to get off the train and throw nickels and dimes to them. When I tell him, this reminds me of throwing peanuts to the monkeys at the zoo in Winnipeg, he laughs and I feel ashamed of the comparison. We head across the tracks and come to three ageing, unpainted sheds. One has no door. Someone carried it off along with the hinges, leaving bleached imprints on the grey wooden frame. Inside, there's nothing but a beat-up bench under the broken window and a rusty metal contraption in one corner. Danny tells me that the vice he has at home came from here.

"You mean you stole it?"

He's defensive. "The mechanics left it behind when they moved to their new workshop. I just helped myself." Back outside, he scrapes around the dwarf willows lining the walls with his shoe. Finding nothing, he turns and saunters towards the largest of the abandoned sheds, which still has a couple of milky windowpanes and a door. He's about to raise the wooden latch when he stops to listen. I stop a step behind him. We can hear laughter and voices inside. One of the voices is all too familiar.

"That's Jeff!"

"I know," Danny replies. He swings the door open slowly and we both stand agape at the scene that greets us. In the middle of the bare, dimly lit space inside, two figures a bit taller than us are hovering over a smaller figure seated on a block of wood.

Had we not heard the voices of the larger pair, it would be hard to recognize them as Jeff and Lennie because of the balaclavas they're wearing. The smaller figure between them is a Chipewyan boy aged eight or nine. They've locked his arms behind his back and gagged him. His eyes open wide when we loom in the doorway. He looks desperate and not at all certain that we can be counted on for help.

"What the hell are you doing?" I challenge Jeff, though it's obvious: he's cutting the boy's hair while Lennie keeps him clamped down on the block of wood. Just as obvious, we've caught them by surprise as complete as our own in an act they'd intended to keep covert. Yet Jeff recovers his composure within seconds when he sees whom they're up against. After hastily concealing the scissors behind his back, he draws them back out while continuing to grip the Chipewyan boy's ear to hold his head straight.

"Well, looky here!" He exclaims, feigning nonchalance at the interruption. "You ever seen these two fellas before, Chester?"

Lennie pretends to look Danny and me up and down in turn. "Can't say I have, Morton. They must be new in town."

Jeff giggles. "Problem with half-breeds is, they all look the same. That other one reminds me of a kid a friend of mine calls Benny Nenny." Pause. "Or is it Benny the Ninny?"

By the way Lennie's eyes are wrinkling, I can tell he has broken into a mocking grin. Next to me, Danny is observing the scene with that deadpan expression I've never been able to decipher. In the meantime, Jeff has let go of the boy's ear and set back to work, yanking hair up tuft by tuft and shearing it off roughly. With each yank the boy winces. His eyes burn with fear and humiliation. My heart is pounding. I struggle to keep my voice level: "You're gonna get into trouble for this."

Jeff lets the tuft of hair he's holding fall and points the half-opened scissors at us menacingly. He imitates a Southern drawl: "Who you think you are, boy, the sheriff?" His eyes, highlighted by the slit of the balaclava, drill into me. My feet are rooted to the floor. I try one last appeal.

"If that kid wanted a haircut..." It's no use. My pluck has dissolved. I hear my voice stammer, as if from a distance, "...he'd go to the barber..." The words trail off feebly.

Jeff snorts and focuses back on his shearing. "I'm the barber here!" he snaps. "I'm gonna teach this here Injun to spread his creepy, crawly cooties all over the school. The little fart gave 'em to my sister!"

Lennie presses down harder on the boy's shoulders. "Don't mind them, buddy," he weighs in. "You're doing' a real fine job."

"You bet I am," Jeff drops another lock of hair into the thickening charcoal-coloured pile at his feet. "And I don't give a fuckin' shit about those two."

I glance at Danny, who continues to look on, silent and noncommittal. The perfect retort to Jeff, namely that the lice were probably home-grown in his family's stinking pigsty, swirls in my head. Yet I'm powerless to deliver a whit of it. My arms hang dead at my sides. All I can do is stare as Jeff crisscrossed the boy's head with the scissors, cropping off every last bit of hair he can sandwich between the blades. When there's nothing left but a ball of uneven black stubble, I say to myself that now at least the torment is over, they'll slap each other on the shoulder and turn the poor wretch loose. But no—Jeff has crueller plans still and the wherewithal to carry them through.

Stepping back, he reaches down for the bottle standing on the floor behind him. There's a greenish liquid inside. While he removes the cap, Lennie tilts the boy's head back, holding him firmly by the chin. Jeff slowly pours the contents of the bottle over the patchy stubble. "Hold still, you little runt!" he warns, shielding the squirming boy's eyes. The muffled cries beneath the gag intensify as the sour-sweet smell of gasoline fills the air. "This'll kill them vile varmints," Jeff hisses. "And I want ya to see what else I got here," he adds fiendishly, setting down the bottle and sliding a hand into his hip pocket. I watch with horror as he removes a book of matches and holds it up with an evil grin. "I wonder what would happen if I lit one of these," he taunts the boy, whose eyes are now stretched wide with terror. It's too much! My dream of the furry little goalie wells up and jars me out of my paralysis.

"You can't do that!" I yell and lunge at Jeff, knocking him off balance as he wasn't expecting the charge. But he's bigger and heavier than me and before I realize what's happening, he has me flailing in a bear hug. Throwing me down, he pins me to the floor, spits in my face and is starting to give me a good workover, with plenty of verbal abuse into the bargain, when suddenly he yelps, his head jerks, his whole body goes limp and he slumps on top of me. Danny has hit him square on the temple with a small silver ball from his slingshot, knocking him unconscious. With my head still spinning, I manage to pull myself out from under him and stagger to my feet. Recovering my senses, I turn to face Lennie, who by this time has released the Chipewyan boy and is grappling with Danny, struggling to wrench the slingshot from his grasp. Now it's Lennie who has pushed Danny to the floor and is pinning him down. I snatch up the scissors, circle behind them, clamp one hand over Lennie's throat and with the other press the point of the scissors into his back.

"Get off of him!" I holler. Lennie tries to shake me off while continuing to hold Danny down with his knees. I drive the scissors harder between two ribs. He screams, jumps to his feet and wheels on me, grabbing for the scissors. But now Danny is up too and has drawn his knife. The blade glints in the wan sunlight streaming through the doorway. Seeing it, Lennie relents and backs off one step at a time.

"You guys'll pay for this," he glowers, out of breath, pulling his balaclava down to wipe his nose with the back of his hand. When he bends down to inspect Jeff, who is still lying prostrate on the floor of rough planks, I wince at the small blood stain on the back of his shirt. Danny and I exchange nervous glances. It's time to clear out.

"Do you think Jeff will be okay?" I wonder as we hurry across the tracks. The boy with the shorn hair is nowhere to be seen. The other Chipewyan kids who were hanging around the station have vanished as well.

"He was breathing, I shot hard but not too hard."

"I held back with the scissors, too." Pause. "You're not worried about the police, are you?"

The lines of his face harden. "Those pricks had it coming and they know it."

We part in front of my house, agreeing to keep mum about the whole business and see what develops. I clasp Danny by the shoulder as we're saying goodbye.

"Thanks, eh. I thought you were gonna stay out of it."

Again that inscrutable expression, though this time with words and a gesture to help interpret it: "With anybody else I would've kept out." He lays a hand over mine for a second before lifting them both from his shoulder and turns away. So, this is how it feels to be comrades in arms, I smile to myself as he trudges down the road to the Flats.

I hole up in my room all day Sunday, eaten by anxiety. On Monday I dread the summons to Mr. McAllister's office that doesn't come. Because of our staggered schedules, we don't see Jeff or Lennie at recess. According to Danny's contacts in the upper grades, he tells me after lunch, Jeff is blaming his bruised forehead on a table corner. I wait for Robin after school at the spot where Danny and I parted on Saturday. A couple of discreet inquiries suggest that no one has informed the police about the haircut. Even so, I can't shake off my trepidation. I decide to lay out the case to Robin in confidence and ask for his advice, knowing he'll relish the chance to hone his skills as a future investigator. I'm not mistaken; he stops me frequently to determine the exact words, actions and positions of the participants at every stage of the altercation.

"Assault with a weapon, causing bodily harm," he summarizes when I'm done. "Have you told your dad?"

"No! I was waiting to see if anyone went to the police before…"

"Then don't!" he interrupts. "Those are both indictable offences."

I have no idea what this means but it sounds perilous. "What about the matches?" I counter, gulping. "If he'd lit one…"

Robin cuts me off again with a wave of his hand. "He didn't. Don't you see, he was just having some fun?"

I stare at him, flabbergasted: "You call that having fun!"

He looks at me pityingly, as if to say, "You ought to become a social worker or some other kind of do-gooder." Still, he remains professional. "Listen, you can't prove anything about their intentions. On the other hand, they've got marks to prove bodily harm."

"Well, so has the kid. He's got no more hair."

Robin hasn't overlooked this point, despite his apparent disregard. "That's what it comes down to," he concedes, concluding the hearing. "If the kid's parents come forward, there'll be trouble for all of you." Pause. "For Danny especially, and you know why." He glances at his watch. "Sorry, I'm supposed to see Cynthia at the Hudson in a few minutes."

My heart stops. "You mean… You two have a date?"

"Yeah, sort of," he smiles, baring two rows of gleaming teeth. God, he's good looking! Is he gloating at my hurt expression? "She wants to hear about Niagara Falls and some other places I visited this summer."

"Niagara Falls…"

"See you 'round."

He leaves me standing there, stultified, my indignation rising. I feel like a lamppost that has just been pissed on. With no hope of redress, because I'm just a poor, dumb lamppost.

As it turns out, the parents don't come forward. I learn from Janie that when the boy refused to go to school with shorn hair, his grandparents took him to their fishing camp across the river.

"He'll stay there till it grows back," Janie reassures me in a low voice. Like all the Chipewyan kids, she knows that Danny and I witnessed the haircut but had no part in it. When I ask why the boy's parents haven't made a complaint, Janie explains, somewhat embarrassed, that the father and mother both drink and are afraid of the police. Some things go unreported, she adds in a resentful tone. There are rumours of a young Chipewyan woman getting gang-raped by the Mounties some years ago. Who could she have complained to?

School is very different without Roger, Robin and Jeff as a buffer between me and Miss Sadler (who's stuck in Churchill for another year). Now they're gone, I've moved to the head of the boys' row, right under her huffy, freckled nose. Behind me are the other two sixth-graders, Danny and a fresh arrival named Logan, followed by three fifth-graders; Ryan, Morris and a pudgy squirt named Oscar who annoys us with his infantile manner. We have thus caught up in numbers with the girls this year. The sucky trio up front have been replaced by Cynthia, opposite me, and the perky pair Yana and Carla. Janie, with two Chipewyan fifth-graders, Lillian and Violet as her new charges, has resumed the role of teaching assistant and interpreter that she lost when Moses was taken away. During the first week, the abiding presence of Cynthia helped fill the pits of having Sad Face so close, but since her defection to Robin the mere sight of her sculpted profile across the aisle rankles me to no end. She was snatched away just as we were moving closer and, sadly, the rift is set to widen as I remain stubbornly prepubescent while she begins her transition into womanhood.

Danny is now the undisputed class clown, with Yana and Carla forming his core gallery. They never tire of his colourful repertoire of antics, which include not only normally well-controlled bursts of flatus and eructation but also a range of mimicry, one-liners and extended vocabulary that he picks up from Andrew and his well-travelled fellow Harbours Board workers. One new word that never fails to draw sniggers when Danny looses it is Kohones, the nickname he pinned on Oscar for arriving on the first day of school with a bulging purple and gold bag of marbles hanging over his crotch. Although no one in the class has the slightest notion of Spanish, we all got the joke immediately—everyone, that is, except Miss Sadler who remains baffled and therefore irritated by it.

Danny has moreover found a source of cash thanks to

Oscar's marbles addiction. Marbles are by far the most popular sport among the town's numerous five-to-nine-year-olds, a peewee league of which Oscar is the senior member. A game consists in digging a shallow hole in the dirt and scratching a line ten paces from it, where the players take turns tossing marbles towards the hole and then either flicking their shooter marble with their thumb and forefinger or knocking it from the outer side of one foot with a kick from the other, ('footsies'), the object being to deflect the opponents' target marbles into the hole and keep them. There are several different categories of marbles but four – crystals, cats' eyes, beauties and steelies – predominate. Their relative value is regulated by a system of exchange rates familiar to everyone. Crystals, which sell for a dime a dozen at S&M's and can thus be easily replaced, are regarded by the urchins as cannon fodder. Cats' eyes are likewise fungible and plentiful but not unlimited in number, since they originate outside of town and enter circulation when they're lost by their owners. The most common cats' eyes are worth two crystals, making them less expendable though still cheap. With beauties, the value of individual marbles quickly escalates. Solid colours generally trade for five cats' eyes while beauties with a pattern fetch more. The Neptune, for example, is highly prized for its wispy white whorls on an exquisite turquoise background. It has been won and lost many times. Far rarer are hand-painted beauties that have found their way to Churchill via collectors, though such treasures are only used as shooters and never risked as target marbles. The last category, steelies, were added to the pantheon this summer and are all the rage. They are as opaque as crystals are transparent, both in appearance and value. They form a top-down, seller's market. A market that Danny has cornered as sole supplier.

"Where do you get these things?" I asked when he started hawking them at the end of June.

"They're bearing balls," was all he would say, displaying a handful ranging from pellet size to the equivalent of a boulder marble. I guessed that he was protecting his source for some reason and didn't press the point, though his guardedness made the steelies all the more intriguing. The most popular, I noted, were three quarters of an inch in diameter. What the kids liked was their weight, which made them easier to control than glass marbles on the town's sandy turf. At first, they were used only as shooters by the handful of players who had acquired one. Since school started, however, Danny has increased supply from a trickle to a steady stream while keeping prices buoyant. He has managed to do so not only thanks to the steelies' continuing novelty but also by relying on the baby-faced Oscar, his distributor, to provide feedback on demand. The gambit is working: the better-off kids now indulge in "steelies only" games with stakes five times higher than when "beauties only" are in play.

"Those balls are used by the dozen in rail cars," Dave explained when I pumped him for background information. He followed up with a crash course on bearings and the balls' role in transferring weight to the cars' wheelsets. Halfway through the lesson I stopped listening when it dawned on me: Danny was covering for someone at the railyard.

"It's Jeremy, isn't it?" I tested my hunch a few days ago after witnessing a furtive sale to Oscar at recess. I'd remembered that the dog breeder worked for the CNR as a labourer. "I bet he's pilfering them for you. Is this a new way to pay for your fish?"

"I told you that's my business," Danny turned away with his hands plunged into his pants pockets. He's been avoiding me since, showing up for school at the last-minute, morning and afternoon, and heading home in stubborn silence as soon as we're let out. What's more, he has been looking bleary-eyed for some time, as if he was up half the night. Today after school, I stop him before he can slip away.

"What's eating you?"

"Nothin'," he tries to brush past me. I grab his arm.

"Come on," I insist. "You know I can keep my mouth shut." He continues to avoid my gaze, his brow dark and furled, his jaw set tightly. "I thought we were friends," I hear myself whining and feel embarrassed. For a moment, I half expect him to beat me off like a maddening horsefly. But if he's angry it's not with me. He squeezes his eyelids together as if concentrating to drive out an inner demon. The tenseness in his arm slackens ever so gradually, then abruptly.

"Okay, but not here," he beckons me to follow. We cross La Verendrye Street, skirting Jeff's house and Caribou Hall. He doesn't speak until we reach the beach. "I got called into the principal's office after lunch." He picks up a large pebble, flings it far out over the water. Seagulls screech overhead. So, that's why he came late to class and ignored the girls' whispered pleas for entertainment all afternoon. Anxiety gushes within me.

"Was it because of the fight?" Three weeks have gone by and although nothing came of it finally, the threat of an unexpected backlash lurks like a bogeyman in the shadows. I've steered clear of Jeff and Lennie, fearing the promise of payback.

"No, it's something else," he turns and starts picking a path over the rocks towards the east. For once, he's moving at a pace he knows I can handle, enabling him to keep talking in his laconic, unhurried manner. "He warned me about hanging around the railyard."

"McAllister?"

"Yeah."

"You mean they don't want you scavenging anymore? Why should they bother about old nuts and bolts?"

"It was the night watchman." Danny's voice has flattened. "He spotted me near the repair hall last week. It was after dark and I ran for it but he thinks he recognized me."

I give him a hard look. "What were you doing in the railyard at night?" He doesn't answer. "Was it for steelies?" I catch a glimpse of Dinosaur Rock to our right, the bird-like head poised in its immemorial bow to drink.

"You were right about Jeremy. He was pinching them for me."

"Whaddya mean, he 'was'?"

"He left town. He found a better job in Gillam and moved away at the end of August. With his dogs."

I think of the increasing numbers of steelies I've seen the kids playing with lately. "Don't tell me you've been pinching them yourself since he left?"

Danny won't admit it straight away. "That day I took you with me to the old sheds... I was still... Whaddya call it when you nose around to get the layout of an area?"

"Reconnoitring. They do that in the army."

"Yeah, I needed to get the distances between the sheds straight in my head before I came back alone. At night." He pauses. "It wasn't hard. Jeremy told me where to go as a last favour."

I picture Danny slinking around the cavernous railyard buildings after dark and am dismayed: "Did you break in?"

"No!" he protests. "They leave a side door of the repair hall unlocked so anyone who needs tools or fasteners or other small stuff can help themselves. They've got tons of those balls, by size, in a big chest. I've been taking a few at a time so nobody'll notice they've gone missing."

We continue on in silence, stopping at last on a tall, flat boulder at the water's edge. Only when Danny sits down on the level surface, crossing his ankles, do I realize we're on Bloody Altar. I kneel down beside him.

"I'm not scared about the watchman." His voice steadies as he eyes the two ships that ride still at anchor in the distance, waiting for a berth at the dock. "I know what days he has off, and his replacement just listens to his short-wave radio all night." Pause. "I'm more worried about McAllister. I told him it wasn't me in the railyard that night but I'm not sure he believed me." Another pause. "He teaches science. If he found out about the steelies, he could put two and two together."

I look at him gravely. "So, you're gonna stop... Right?" He gives me no answer. I can see he's battling with his conscience.

"Don't you see?" he turns to me, finally, almost pleading. "It's not fair. Every time I try and get somewhere, it's as if they're waiting to trip me up."

"Stealing's dishonest," I counter meekly.

"So was shooting my dog!" A tear rolls down his cheek. He wipes it away. "Oscar's starting to sell steelies by the dozen at the Fort. At this rate I can make ten bucks a week! I gotta keep this thing going while it lasts. It'll be snowing soon and the kids'll pack in their marbles."

"That's a lot of money," I whistle. "But you're asking for it."

"Not if I play it right." His jaw is thrust forward again.

The wind is picking up as dusk starts to set in. I'm shivering and afraid of slipping on the way back. I remind Danny it will soon be suppertime.

"I'm gonna stay and think a while," he murmurs, still gazing fixedly out over the water.

I pick my way back over the rocks with great care, the twisted shapes looming stark and gloomy around me. A ghostly overlay looms in my mind: an image of Danny being called before Dad, head bowed, hands stuffed in his pockets, charged with theft. Where did he get his maverick streak? He knows damn well he's in hot water and still he seems bent on wading in deeper.

Worse, he's about to walk into a trap the details of which I won't find out until after the whole painful episode is over. It began recently when Jeff, who's a keen observer, couldn't help noticing the sudden spread of steelies. Not that he takes any interest in the peewee league's marbles games, but remembering that Danny had used the same type of ball to knock him out in the railyard shed, he was keen to find out where they were coming from. Tracing their source as far as Oscar was easy. The little shrimp at first tried to cover for Danny, on his instructions, but he quickly spilled the beans when Jeff lifted him up by the lapels of his jacket, spat in his face and threatened to hurl him head-first into a nearby puddle.

"That smart-ass half-breed's got a racket going!" Jeff fulminated to Lennie the next day after lunch. They were standing near the steps of the main school building,

"Sounds like sandbox racketeering to me," Lennie sniffed.

"I tell you he's making a killing!" Jeff insisted, consumed with hate and jealousy. "Look at 'em!" It was a few minutes before one p.m. when all the primary and secondary grades were milling in the schoolyard, waiting for Miss Spencer to come out and ring the bell. Jeff had spotted Danny and Oscar disappear together behind our trailer while the rest of us were queuing up to go into class.

"You're sure we're talking about real money, not pennies and nickels?" Lennie queried. His eyes were on the pair as they came sauntering back a moment later.

"Fifty cents apiece. The asshole's raking it in!"

Lennie's expression turned serious. "Then we might have him where we want him," he said slowly, "If we can be sure they're inside the school grounds and somebody can catch them in the act."

"I can watch for them from my place and still make it here for the bell," Jeff proposed. Which he did, spying from inside the porch of his house across the street until he witnessed another exchange two days ago.

"It was on this side of the street, just in bounds!" he reported triumphantly.

"Then it's time for payback," Lennie smiled slyly and proceeded to lay out the plan he'd been devising. It required proper timing and showmanship on Jeff's part. The right moment to put it into action would be tomorrow night, when Jeff's father comes home suitably drunk and ornery from his weekly binge.

Jeff waits up for him on the living room sofa, reading the sports section of last week's *Toronto Star*. He peers over the headline *Habs Ready for New Season* as the janitor staggers in from the porch and slumps down in his armchair spotted with cigarette burns.

"You sure tied one on tonight, didn't you?" He tries to sound grown-up, a tad comradely, laying down the paper. "Must be fun at the beer parlour." A loud belch reeking of Molson ale is all he receives for an answer. That's all he was expecting: the janitor doesn't speak when he's still stewing in his juices. Jeff knows from experience, however, that under the fog of inebriation he's listening. "More fun than cleaning up after the kids at school…

With all the dirt they drag in... after playing marbles," Jeff begins to bait him. "Have you noticed lately? They're playing with metal marbles, more and more. They've gone bonkers over them." The janitor frowns. "Some games end in a fist fight, with one little jerk accusing the other of cheating—nudging his shooter half an inch while setting up. Nothing new about that, but now they're tearing each other apart. Never used to happen!" The janitor sniffs, rubs his runny nose on the sleeve of his tattered sweater. "It's because of the money. They're spending wads of it – their whole allowances – on these steelies, they're called... A kid got caught stealing from his dad's wallet to buy one, can you imagine that? Couldn't stand being left out." There's a deep rumble of indignation. Jeff waits to make sure the next revelation will strike home as well. "It's that no-good half-breed Danny who's selling them. He must be making a bundle, at fifty cents apiece." Bingo! The janitor's face is tinged with yellow, a sure sign that his gall bladder has kicked into overdrive. If there are two things he can't tolerate, it's kids and Indians with money.

"Fifty cents apiece!" he roars to Mr. McAllister on Monday morning. "While I'm here bustin' my ass carryin' out their slop!" His bloodshot eyes are flaming. "It's that stinkin', connivin' half-breed—"

"Métis."

"—Danny what's behind it! He's got the kids so goddamn fired up with them things, they're robbin' their parents to buy 'em! Can you imagine?"

The principal is used to the janitor's railing. He listens dispassionately, smoothing his pencil moustache and looking at his watch. He's about to interrupt when the janitor ends his spluttering rant with a wager (on Jeff's prompting) that Danny is up to his no-good business right under their noses, on the school grounds. McAllister's features instantly harden: a red line may have been crossed. "Fifty-cent marbles ... That's indeed beyond the means of the town's young children," he concedes. "And I agree most firmly ... The school is out of bounds for vending of any sort." With time running out before class, he promises that Danny will be severely punished if he's caught trafficking within the school perimeter. At this point, he hasn't guessed the connection between the steelies and the CNR watchman's denunciation.

"The jig's up!" Jeff rubs his hands together after briefing Lennie on his father's account of the scene with McAllister.

Lennie remains cagey: "We can't pull the trigger yet, not till we get them right in our sights." He pauses. "But I have an idea... A guy I play baseball with at the Fort says those steelies have started showing up there too. That means the squirt must be pushing his hardware on the kids' playground, next to the ball diamond. I'll keep my eyes peeled for him during our game against the Fort team this Saturday..."

Jeff is pawing the ground impatiently on Monday morning when Lennie arrives at the steps of the main school building. "Did you see him dealing?"

"You bet I did! He must've sold a couple dozen of those balls. That means he's loaded!"

"Then today's the day to nail him, we'll do it when they meet after lunch. I'll tell my dad."

And so it is that, come five to one, Jeff's father has alerted the principal, who can't go back on his word. While Logan and I stand in line talking, the two approach in lockstep – the principal grim-faced, the janitor concealing a smile – and walk past us round the back of our trailer.

A few minutes later, inside, we're pulling out our math books when Danny and Oscar enter from the back. Miss Sadler, who is standing up front preparing to berate the two latecomers before launching into the sixth-grade lesson, is startled by the appearance of the principal behind them. She pushes up her glasses, waiting for him to speak first.

"Please be seated, Miss Sadler!" Mr. McAllister calls from the back while Danny and Oscar take off their coats and walk silently to their desks. "I have something to say to the class." The iciness of his tone strikes fear into me and I'm not alone, judging by the inertness of my classmates. As he strides up the aisle on the girls' side, my heart begins to pound apace. It's a replay of the afternoon almost a year ago when he came to announce President Kennedy's assassination. Only, this time, I've realized the purpose of his visit.

"Boys and girls," his salutation rings harshly, "I'm here to remind you …" again, with staccato phrasing, "…that school is not a place of business." His grey eyes pan our faces. "I've just caught Danny and Oscar in an exchange of money… for these." He produces three steelies from the pocket of his corduroy jacket, holding them out in the palm of his hand for all to see. "Now, Oscar…" his gaze travels over my head to the back of the boys' row, "I'm letting you off with a stern warning… Never to do this… or any other kind of trafficking… on the school grounds again! Is that clear?" There's a long silence punctuated by Oscar's faint "Yes, Sir" four desks behind mine. "But the instigator, I know…" McAllister is now addressing all of us, "…was Danny… who seems to have no respect… for authority!" I can feel myself sweating. My cheeks are burning. "Miss Sadler… The strap, please!"

My heart freezes. The dreaded band of leather hasn't been used on any of us since the mayhem in Bible reading a year ago.

The expectation that it's about to be administered by the principal himself is all the more harrowing. As Miss Sadler opens the middle drawer of her desk, I again feel the revulsion of seeing it lying there; black and scaly, almost under my nose. Now she has lifted it out, stood up and is walking to hand it to McAllister. The way it dangles by her side brings back another hideous scene, this summer, when my cousin Jim and his family came to the farm for a visit. To my horror, Jim cornered a snake in the pump house and stamped on its tail before it could dart away.

"Let's kill it!" he exclaimed with gleeful anticipation, picking it up skilfully behind the head with his thumb and forefinger. Fighting back my phobia, I followed him up the dirt driveway, keeping on his left side while he let the thing dangle, hissing vociferously, from his right hand. When we got to the gate, I lifted the wire loop holding it down and the bucket of heavy stones at the other end sank, causing the crossbars to swing up. We went through and he flung the snake down on the gravel road beyond, pinning it in place with a rock. We then proceeded to flatten the thing end to end by dropping more heavy stones on top of it. Until its guts spewed out of its yawning mouth, well after it lay still.

"Danny, come up here!" McAllister orders. I hear a rustle behind me as Danny hesitates, then swings out of his desk onto his feet. He walks by me slowly, head bowed, hands plunged into his pants pockets.

"Head up and look at me!" The edge on the principal's voice has sharpened. "Hands out of your pockets!" You could hear a pin drop. Cynthia, across from me, is looking down at her ivory hands clasped on her open math book. Miss Sadler is looking away. So am I.

"Left hand!" McAllister grips the arm Danny proffers

reluctantly, turns the palm of his hand upward, pushes back the shirt cuff to bare his wrist and delivers ten resounding smacks, raising the strap the full length of his arm before bringing it down. Danny flinches but stands his ground, silent. "Right hand!" Again, ten blows to the wrist that draw whimpers this time. I sneak a glance through the fingers covering my eyes when it's over. Danny's trembling, fighting back tears.

"Now take your coat and leave, mister!" McAllister barks, holding the strap like a smoking gun at his hip. "You're suspended from school till I've determined where these balls come from!" Danny's head is bowed again, his eyes glistening. He turns and trudges past me, the principal's glare following him down the aisle. I hear him tear his jacket off the coatrack, wrench open the trailer door and, in a final act of defiance, stalk out without closing it.

"Oscar, shut the door!" McAllister orders, continuing to stand facing us up front. He's going to turn this into a lecture, I say to myself. And he does, clearing his throat for rhetorical effect once Oscar has returned to his seat. "You kids today need to listen more... to authority!" He emphasizes the last word. "You've got too much of everything... Toys, distractions, free time... Too much freedom, not enough drive!" A long pause. "Drive," he repeats the word thoughtfully. "Time was... we had nothing... No money... no work... When we finished school, young men like me had three choices: the Army, the Air Force or the Navy..." His staccato bursts start to flow. "I joined an armoured car regiment, the 12th Manitoba Dragoons... We fought our way out of Normandy, through Belgium and Holland, into Germany..." His grey eyes grow misty. "I can tell you about drive, about blood and guts... If you ever have a chance to visit the town of Bruges, in Flanders, you'll find a bridge... the

Canada Bridge, flanked by two huge, bronze bison… In our honour!" Another long pause. "The freedom you squander today… we won it for you… by doing our duty… By heeding authority!" His steely gaze pans us once more, for good measure. "Now it's time for you to get down to work… Show us what you're capable of!" He hands the strap back to Miss Sadler and marches out without a goodbye.

Like last time, he leaves a pall of uneasiness behind him. It's a while before my cheeks cool and my heartbeat returns to normal. Still, I can't focus. I feel Danny's absence, the numbing emptiness of his desk behind me. The afternoon drags by, as if it were pulling a tremendous weight. When four o'clock comes at last and we're allowed to leave one by one, I dash home and stash my binder in the front porch, freeing my hands to clamber over the rocks towards the east. The bay is bleak and empty, the last ships departed. There's a fierce nip in the air, a harbinger of our first snowfall in the coming days. I find Danny where I knew he would be, huddled on Bloody Altar, gazing out over the dark water. He doesn't turn when I join him.

"Those welts must hurt," I murmur, eyeing the angry red streaks on the underside of his wrists. He hides them by crossing his arms on his knees and slouches forward. I try prodding him out of his sullen silence. "What's your mom gonna say… About the suspension?"

He continues to stare ahead. "She'll be pissed off," he says finally, with a long sigh. "She'll cry and tell me again how she would've liked to stay in school. How they put her to work at fourteen." I think of his mother upbraiding him with her French accent, wringing her small hands calloused from scrub boards and laundry soap, her soft, doe-like eyes filled with tears. "She warned me about staying out at night. So did Andrew."

There's no sense in me continuing in that direction. It's a dead end. I try another tack: "What do you like about this rock? What makes you come here?"

To my surprise, he's forthcoming. "I can talk to it," he half whispers. I crouch closer to hear him above the splashing of the waves below.

"More than to people?"

"Yeah, something like that."

"And it listens? It doesn't tell you you have to go school, follow the rules? Take shit from a drunken bigot of a janitor and a principal who thinks driving a tank across Europe made him a hero?"

Danny looks me straight in the eye—startled, it seems, that I have an inkling of what goes on in his head. I want to tell him it's because he has allowed me a peek, for the first time. If I knew now what I'll know twenty-five years on, I could tell him a lot more. The real story of this rock, for starters: that the red blotch at its base is a birthmark, not a stain.

"So, what's Bloody Altar saying to you now?"

He has turned his gaze away again, out over the gunmetal grey expanse of the bay. "It's saying… That maybe I shouldn't raise sled dogs after all… Or only for a while … That I should think about going to sea."

Printed by BoD in Norderstedt, Germany